"Sue, I just need a word with Lila," Declan said quickly.

"That won't be necessary, Doctor." Pointedly Lila pulled her arm away.

"No, you two go right ahead," Sue said brightly, ignoring Lila's desperate eye signals. "I'll buzz if things pick up out here."

They ended up in Hester's office, Lila's cheeks burning with anger and the strangest awareness at finding herself finally alone with him. As Declan closed the door he turned slowly, his face serious. Suddenly, he looked older, so much older than the carefree young man she had once known.

"You finished with me," he said, as if that last couple of minutes had never happened. "You were the one who ended two years with a single phone call. Who packed up and moved without leaving a forwarding address. Hell, I've still got a box of records and clothes you left at my place, makeup and jewelry you left on my dressing table, which you never came back for." His voice was rising now, and Lila was stunned to hear the pain behind it. "And you think you're the one that got hurt?"

Dear Reader,

Perhaps you are driving home one evening when you spot a rotating flashing light or hear a siren. Instantly, your pulse quickens—it's human nature. You can't help responding to these signals that there is an emergency somewhere close by.

Heartbeat, romances being published in North America for the first time, brings you the fast-paced kinds of stories that trigger responses to life-and-death situations. The heroes and heroines, whose lives you will share in this exciting series of books, devote themselves to helping others, to saving lives, to *caring*. And while they are devotedly doing what they do best, they manage to fall in love!

Since these books are largely set in the U.K., Australia and New Zealand, and mainly written by authors who reside in those countries, the medical terms originally used may be unfamiliar to North American readers. Because we wanted to ensure that you enjoyed these stories as thoroughly as possible, we've taken a few special measures. Within the stories themselves, we have substituted American terms for British ones we felt would be very unfamiliar to you. And we've also included in these books a short glossary of terms that we've left in the stories, so as not to disturb their authenticity, but that you might wonder about.

So prepare to feel your heart beat a little faster! You're about to experience love when life is on the line!

Yours sincerely,

Marsha Zinberg,
Executive Editor, Harlequin Books

LOVESICK
Carol Marinelli

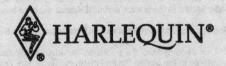

HARLEQUIN®

TORONTO • NEW YORK • LONDON
AMSTERDAM • PARIS • SYDNEY • HAMBURG
STOCKHOLM • ATHENS • TOKYO • MILAN • MADRID
PRAGUE • WARSAW • BUDAPEST • AUCKLAND

ISBN 0-373-51253-8

LOVESICK

First North American Publication 2003

Copyright © 2002 by Carol Marinelli

Carol Marinelli is a nurse who loves writing. Or is she a writer who loves nursing? The truth is Carol's having trouble deciding at the moment, but writing definitely seems to be taking precedence! She's also happily married to an eternally patient husband (an essential accessory when panic hits around chapter six) and is a mother to three fabulously boisterous children. Add would-be tennis player, eternal romantic and devout daydreamer to that list and that pretty much sums Carol up. Oh, she's also terrible at housework!

GLOSSARY

A and E—accident and emergency department

B and G—bloods and glucose

Consultant—an experienced specialist registrar who is the leader of a medical team; there can be a junior and senior consultant on a team

CVA—cerebrovascular accident

Duty registrar—the doctor on call

FBC—full blood count

Fixator—an external device, similar to a frame, for rigidly holding bones together while they heal

GA—general anesthetic

GCS—the Glasgow Coma Scale, used to determine a patient's level of consciousness

Houseman/house officer—British equivalent of a medical intern or clerk

MI—myocardial infarction

Obs—observations re: pulse, blood pressure, etc.

Registrar/specialist registrar—a doctor who is trained in a particular area of medicine

Resus—room or unit where a patient is taken for resuscitation after cardiac accident

Rostered—scheduled

Rota—rotation

RTA—road traffic accident

Senior House Officer (SHO)—British equivalent of a resident

Theatre—operating room

PROLOGUE

'I KNOW this is terrible news, Lila.' Dr Mason gave her a sympathetic smile. 'But at least now you know the reason for your mother's mood swings and confusion.'

'But Alzheimer's!' Lila closed her eyes, battling with tears. She had been doing a lot of reading on the subject since Alzheimer's had been gently suggested as a possible diagnosis, and none of the books, none of the statistics, had given her even a shred of comfort. 'How long—how long until…?'

'Alzheimer's is a progressive disorder, but, as the neurologist would have explained to you when he first referred your mother for tests, the progression of the disease varies in each individual. It could be months, it could be years. However…' The pause as Dr Mason searched for the right words seemed interminable, yet Lila found herself wishing he would stop right there. Stop before he took away her last ray of hope. 'In your mother's case the progress has been rather rapid. Elizabeth is already at the stage where she requires some degree of supervision, and I'm sorry to say that isn't going to improve. Now, I know that what with your job and everything—'

'I'll sort something out,' Lila interrupted quickly.

'Lila, you're a flight attendant,' Dr Mason pointed out. 'Your mother needs round-the-clock supervision; she really can't be left alone.'

'Well, I'll give up the long-haul flights and switch to domestic. My aunt will help out while I'm working. She said she would, if the news was bad.'

'Short term, maybe. Look, Lila, I don't know your aunt, and I'm sure her intentions are good, but we're talking months—years, even—of care for your mother. At some point you're going to have to think about a home.'

'No!' The single word spilled from her lips forcefully. 'Look, I know you're a doctor, and I know you think you know how it will end up, but this is my mother we're talking about, and she's *not* going into a home. I'm going to look after her.'

Dr Mason didn't push; he was more of a family friend than a GP. He had delivered Lila into the world twenty-three years ago. He had seen her through inoculations and ear infections, and later acne and all the usual teenage angst. He could remember her shyly coming into his office to discuss contraception, her face glowing as she spoke about her beloved Declan. He had watched her grow from a cheeky, chubby baby with a mass of blonde curls into a groomed, jet-setting woman. Seeing her sitting there now, with a pained, dignified look on her face as she struggled to come to terms with the terrible news, he felt her pain too.

Still cheeky, though, he thought affectionately as he fiddled with his fountain pen. Still impulsive, and still with a heart of gold. Dr Mason loved his job most of the time, but on days like this…

'Look, you don't have to make any decision today; this is a long haul we're talking about here. I just feel you'd be better prepared if you at least start to address some of the issues that are likely to present themselves. Looking after your mum at home is going to be a big deal. We're talking full-time care, lifting, feeding and washing. Unless you can afford a caregiver, unless you've got a lot of support, you're simply not going to be able to do it.'

'I'll work something out.'

Dr Mason watched Lila gather her bag. 'I've got together some literature for you to read once you get your breath back,' he said gently. 'There're also the numbers of some support groups that you might like to contact.'

'I'll see.' Standing, Lila shook Dr Mason's hand. 'Thank you for being so honest; I know this can't have been easy.'

'I'll call round in a couple of days.' Opening the consulting-room door, he saw the flash of tears in her eyes as she brushed past him. 'I am sorry, Lila. I just wish it could have been better news.'

* * *

Declan tried to be sympathetic when she told him, but his fifth year medical student brain simply wasn't up to the questions Lila kept hurling at him.

'Lila, you're jumping the gun,' he responded when Lila threatened to resign from the airline. 'The doctor said, it could be years—you don't have to throw in your job.'

'Someone has to look after her.'

'Of course, but you need to work. Surely your aunt—'

'I can't expect Shirley to just give up her life and look after her sister.'

He ran an exasperated hand through his long dark curls, screwing his grey eyes closed for a second as he tried to take in the enormity of the news Lila had just divulged. He knew he should stay calm, be the strong one, support her decisions. But he couldn't just let her destroy her life, and the Lila he knew and loved was more than capable of doing just that!

Her impulsive nature was one of the things he loved about her most. But, seeing her standing there in his living room, about to make all the wrong decisions, he had to step in—had to stop Lila in her tracks and make her see sense.

'You haven't even spoken to her about it,' he reasoned. 'Once the news has sunk in then we can all sit down and work something out. If you won't listen to me, then listen to what Dr Mason said: ''You don't have to make any decisions today." He's right. When you go home your mum's going to be there, just as she was this morning; the only difference is that now you know what's wrong. Don't go handing in your notice or doing anything rash.'

But his words fell on deaf ears.

'What if I studied nursing? I'd be living at home then, and by the time Mum needs full-time care I'd at least know what I was doing.' She was clutching at straws now, throwing up ideas, trying anything to gain control of this awful situation.

'You? Nurse? Oh, come on, Lila. All the nurses I've come across are organised, dedicated—they don't just decide on a Tuesday morning that nursing is the job for them. They have a vocation, a passion for it. You're the scattiest person I know—not that I love you any less for it—and the only thing you're dedicated to is international shopping. For heaven's sake, darling, you don't even like the sight of blood!' Maybe it was helplessness, maybe it was a feeble attempt to lighten the mood, but when Declan committed the cardinal sin of laughing at the idea Lila turned promptly on her heel.

'Lila, don't walk off.' Declan followed her out to the hall. 'Don't leave while you're upset. Come on, we need to talk about this—we need to work something out.'

'That,' retorted Lila, her words filled with venom,

her eyes blazing, 'was what I was trying to do. You get back to your books, Declan, and leave me to get on with my life.'

Slamming the door on the town house Declan shared with his fellow students, Lila marched off, safe in the knowledge he wouldn't run after her, given the fact he was dressed only in boxer shorts.

'Lila!'

Flemington Road was amongst the busiest in Melbourne. Lila wasn't the only one to look shocked as he raced along the pavement after her.

'Come back inside—please,' he begged, oblivious of the curious stares of onlookers.

A tram was approaching and Lila flagged it down, scrabbling in her bag for her travel card.

'Lila!' His voice was urgent now.

'Goodbye, Declan.'

As the tram moved off she willed herself not to turn around but sat there rigid, her eyes trained on the driver in front. The old lady sitting next to her had no such reserve, though. Craning her neck, she gave Lila an unwelcome update as the tram turned right at the roundabout.

'He's still there, God love him, just standing there in his undies. You've given him a scare, love, why don't you get off now and go back to him?'

What was it with Australians? Why did they have to be so damned friendly? Why couldn't she live in

London, where people sat on the underground and pretended not to notice someone fainting?

'There's no point,' Lila said flatly, tears welling in her eyes as the full enormity of the situation hit her. There really was no point at all. Sure, if she got off now they'd make up—he'd take her in his arms and tell her it would all be all right, that he loved her and would always be there for her. But how could he make a promise like that when there was so much uncertainty ahead? The Lila Bailey he loved was independent, with a job to die for and a wardrobe to match. How would he feel when she was stuck at home, nursing her mother, who, with even the best will in the world, was only going to get worse?

As she walked in the front door she braced herself, unsure of what she would find today. The bathroom flooded? A burning pot on the stove, perhaps? Instead, her mother was dozing peacefully in the armchair, her eyes flicking open as Lila made her way across the room.

'Hello, darling, how was the flight?'

'I haven't been at work, Mum. I just went to see Declan.'

Elizabeth screwed up her nose. 'Frightful young man. He can't be trusted, you know. He's exactly like your father. And we all know how that turned out.'

Standing, she smiled warmly at her daughter. 'You

have a seat, dear, and put your feet up. I'll see about getting you a nice cup of tea and perhaps some cake.'

Slipping into the chair, Lila felt herself start to relax. Maybe Declan was right and she *was* jumping the gun. Mum was fine. It could be years down the track…

'How was Singapore?' Elizabeth asked, returning moments later with a cup of hot sugared water. 'You must be exhausted after such a long flight.'

It was on that day Lila rang to make enquiries about applying to study for a Bachelor of Nursing.

It was on that day she finished with Declan.

CHAPTER ONE

LILA burst into the observation ward, her blonde hair flying, her bag falling off her shoulder.

'Calm down, they haven't started yet.' Sue Finch patted the chair beside her. 'I saved you a seat.'

'Don't you hate that?' Lila rolled her eyes. 'They tell us to be here at eight—an hour before our shift starts—and then they can't even get it started on time.'

'Just as well or you'd have been late—again.' Sue grinned. 'Luckily the Horse is stuck round in Resus, so your lack of punctuality will go unnoticed—this time,' she added pointedly.

The Horse was the name Hester Randall, the nurse unit manager, was unaffectionately known by, due to the fact that the only time she showed any glimpse of being human was when she spoke about one of her beloved horses. Lila had started the nickname after a particularly bad dressing-down from her senior and it had soon caught on. 'What kept you, anyway?'

'I started watching the gymnastics on television, and before I knew it it was after seven.'

15

'Since when have you been interested in gymnastics?' Sue asked.

'Since a couple of hours ago. I don't know what all the fuss is about—it doesn't look that difficult. I'm sure if I practised I could do it.' She laughed at Sue's incredulous look. 'I'm serious. They were just dancing around waving a couple of ribbons.'

'They practise for years—hours every day,' Lucy Heath, another of the night nurses, pointed out.

'Exactly my point.' Flicking back the curtains pulled around the empty ward and seeing the coast was clear, Lila picked up a couple of finger bandages and unravelled them. 'Watch and learn,' she said to her delighted audience, and, executing a perfect pirouette, she twirled the ribbons as she danced around the room, egged on by the laughter coming from her colleagues. Too wrapped up in her impromptu routine, she didn't notice the laughter had suddenly changed to a fit of embarrassed coughing.

'When you've finished wasting the hospital supplies, Nurse Bailey, perhaps we can get on with the evening's lecture?'

Turning, Lila stopped in her tracks, her face turning pale as Hester Randall marched in, accompanied by a couple of medical personnel. Lila took her seat next to Sue, concentrating on rolling the bandages—anything rather than look up. It wasn't Hester's untimely appearance that had upset her; Lila was far too used to that by now. The trembling in her hands, the rapid rise in her heart rate, were exclusively due to the, oh, so familiar grin that had greeted Lila's eyes as she'd spun around.

'Before we start I'd like to take a moment to introduce two new faces that are soon going to become very familiar to us all. Yvonne Selles is the hospital's new geriatric registrar, and will be delivering tonight's talk. Yvonne has moved to Melbourne all the way from Scotland, so I trust you will do your utmost to make her feel welcome. The other new face belongs to Dr Declan Haversham, our new emergency registrar. Theoretically he shouldn't be starting for another month, but as you know we are short of a night doctor for the next few weeks, and Declan has agreed to step in.'

Lila had known this day would come—that one day their paths would cross again. But the eight years that had elapsed since their last meeting, or rather parting, had almost convinced her that she was worrying unnecessarily. Almost convinced her that maybe she could get through the rest of her life without coming face to face with Declan.

It was no big deal, Lila tried to convince herself as she finished rolling the bandages. It was just an ex-boyfriend—hardly big league stuff; she could handle this!

But it *was* a big deal, she finally acknowledged.

Eight years might have passed, but not a day or night had gone by when Declan hadn't been in her thoughts. His tousled black hair, the grey eyes that crinkled around the edges when he laughed, or softened when he gazed into hers... Correction, Lila reminded herself, the same eyes that had mocked her when she had tentatively told him her plans, and the same cheeky grin that had turned into a scornful laugh.

Peeking up from under her fringe, she saw that he was staring directly at her. Feigning uninterest, Lila flicked her gaze away, but not before she saw a smile tug at the corner of his lips. That small glimpse was enough to tell her the years had treated him well. His hair was shorter, neater now, and he looked even taller, if that was possible. And the suit under his white coat had obviously set him back a bit. His eyes still crinkled, though, she mused, desperately trying to focus on Yvonne Selles's lecture, and nothing could diminish the impact of those eyes on hers...

'My intention is to highlight to the staff here the special needs of elderly patients in the accident and emergency department.' Yvonne's lilting Scottish accent forced the staff to listen more carefully. 'Would any of you like to suggest what specific problems they might face during their time here?'

'Missing out on their regular medication?' Sue suggested.

'Excellent. Their GP will have spent a lot of time educating them, insisting that they take their medication at a certain time, stressing the importance of not missing a dose. The elderly patients might suffer with dementia, might be confused, but they know that at six p.m. they have to take their blue tablet— or their insulin, perhaps. Then they come into Emergency and, lo and behold, a nurse tells them that as it isn't prescribed they can't have it, and, anyway, missing out on one dose isn't going to cause a problem. It can take weeks to undo that sort of damage when in truth it could be so easily prevented. Can anyone suggest how?'

'By getting them seen more quickly, perhaps,' Lila suggested. 'Even if not for a full assessment, at least a doctor could write up an interim order for their regular meds, enabling the staff to give them if required.'

She could feel Declan's eyes on her and couldn't help a small blush as she spoke. It felt surreal, discussing medical issues with him in the room.

'Well done. Any other problem that comes to mind?'

Yvonne was looking directly at her now, and Lila had no choice but to make a suggestion. 'Pressure areas?'

'Another good point. Unlike the wards, the emergency department doesn't have a routine as such.

Emergency staff are busy dealing with the immediate and in some cases life-threatening problem that has caused the patient to present in the first place. So often elderly people lie on hard trolleys without the very basics of nursing care being addressed. By the time they get to the wards damage has been inflicted upon their frail skin. So what can be done?'

It was Lucy who responded this time. 'Implement a system of assessing an elderly patient when they come in—if they need pressure area care then make sure it's carried out regularly.'

'It wouldn't work,' Lila said thoughtfully. 'Maybe for a couple of weeks, but sooner or later everyone would slip back into the old ways. We could start doing four-hourly pressure area rounds, like on the wards. Anybody needing pressure area care would be treated then.'

'A fantastic idea. What do you think, Hester?'

Yvonne turned and addressed the unit manager, who gave a thin smile. 'Worth some thought, I'm sure,' Hester agreed, though her tone could hardly be described as enthusiastic.

The meeting continued in the same vein. They bounced ideas off each other, trying to come up with solutions to the endless problems nursing threw up, but finally at ten to nine they were done, leaving just enough time to grab a quick coffee before the night shift started.

'Thanks a bunch,' Sue said good-naturedly as they picked up their bags. 'If we don't have enough work already, now the Horse will have us doing pressure area rounds. I came down to Emergency to escape all that!'

'Nurse Bailey, if I could have a quick word in my office?' Hester's voice was hardly friendly, and, forgoing any chance of a coffee, Lila turned and followed her boss down the corridor, closing the door behind her as Hester took a seat at her desk.

Anticipating a ticking off for her gymnastic display, Lila tried to keep her face impassive. Her lateness she could accept being told off for—after all, none of the staff knew the true extent of her mother's illness. If they had she was sure they would have happily made allowances. However, Lila consistently refused to apologise for having a bit of fun now and then. Heaven knew, the staff worked hard enough in this department—between them they saw enough terrible sights to send even the most stable person searching their soul. Letting off a bit of steam at work did no harm, in Lila's eyes; in fact, she felt it did a lot of good. It was a point she and Hester would never agree on, and one of the many reasons Lila preferred night duty. Away from the politics of days, away from the bureaucracy and the demands of admin, staff were able to get on with what they were paid to do—nurse.

But for now, at least, the waste of two hospital bandages wasn't what Hester had on her mind.

'I've been going through the applications for the night associate charge nurse position, and I see you're not amongst them.'

As she sat down on the chair Lila's impassive expression slipped for a moment. 'I thought it would be a waste of time,' she admitted honestly, after a moment's silence.

'Why? Don't you want the job?' Hester's voice was crisp, her stare direct, but, undaunted, Lila looked her directly in the eye.

'On the contrary, I'd love the position. However, I know that we don't always see eye to eye on my methods of nursing—'

'Your nursing methods don't worry me,' Hester interrupted. 'I don't doubt for a moment that you're an excellent nurse. If I had any concerns in that area you'd have been gone long ago. What concerns me is your disregard for detail, your casual attitude to the rules, your lateness.'

Which was a backhanded compliment if ever Lila had heard one. Biting back a smart reply, she kept her voice even. 'Which is why I didn't apply for the job.'

Hester didn't answer immediately. Instead, she flicked through the pile of résumés on the desk in front of her. 'All of these are from external applicants. While I don't doubt that their credentials are excellent, and while I agree I don't always see eye to eye with you, Lila, I do think you're a good nurse. I'm also paid to have foresight, and I can't see it going down too well with the rest of your colleagues if I employ an outsider for a job you're effectively already doing.'

Hester had a point there. Since Jane Church had left, more often than not Lila had been in charge of the department, and the rest of the night staff had been pushing endlessly for Lila to apply for the position permanently.

'Now, I'm certainly not going to hand you such a senior position on a plate, but I definitely would seriously consider you if you decided to go ahead and apply. Who knows? When it's you handling the stock-ordering and budgets, maybe a measly couple of bandages might take on a greater importance.'

Lila managed a faintly sheepish grin as Hester continued. 'The applications close tomorrow at five p.m. It's up to you whether your name's amongst them. I'd better let you get back to the unit.'

Making her way back to emergency, Lila shook her head in disbelief. Hester suggesting she apply for the position was the last thing she had been expecting. Correction, Lila thought as she rounded the corner and saw Declan standing by the whiteboard, studying the patient list. Declan Haversham strolling back into her life as, of all things, the newly appointed emergency registrar was the last thing. How on earth was she supposed to deal with this?

As she approached the huddle of nurses, painfully aware of his eyes on her, Lila took a deep breath. It was going to be a long, long night.

As the nurse in charge it was up to Lila to assign the nurses their various roles for the night. It was quite a complicated task. Assessing the patients who were in the department, along with nurses' capabilities, was a constantly evolving juggling act.

'Sue, you take the observation ward, if anyone gets admitted, otherwise stay down in section A with me. For now start shifting some of the patients up to the wards,' Lila said, writing swiftly on the whiteboard as she did so. 'Lucy and Amy, you stay in section A with me, and help Sue. We'll all cover Resuscitation together. Gemma, perhaps you could close section B now and bring the patient list up here. And, girls,' she added, calling back the dispersing group, 'remember your para-training.'

'Will do, Lila.' Sue grinned. 'Hey, what did the Horse want?'

'What do you think she wanted?' Lila said lightly. She certainly wasn't about to divulge the real reason for Hester's little chat. It would be bad enough not getting the job, without every one knowing about it! 'You do realise I cost the hospital four dollars tonight, teaching you Neanderthals the finer points of gymnastics.'

'And a real treat it was, too.'

Lila pointedly didn't look round as Declan came over.

'I never knew you were such a talented gymnast.' She could hear the familiar dry humour in his voice, but still she didn't look. 'But then what would I know? I never even realised you were a nurse.'

Sue gave them both a quizzical look. 'I'll get cubicle four up to the ward, then,' she said, leaving them to it.

For the longest time they stood there, both pretending to study the whiteboard. It was Declan who finally broke the silence. 'So you were serious about nursing after all?'

Lila gave a curt nod. 'It looks that way.'

'I guess you must have got over your weak stomach?'

'Not in the slightest.'

He looked up at her wry chuckle. 'But you work in Emergency!' His voice was incredulous, but Lila was used to shock when she admitted her weakness. Her response was well rehearsed.

'Name one person who loves every aspect of their job.' When he didn't immediately answer Lila jumped right in. 'See, you can't! Emergency isn't just about blood and gore—that's just one aspect of it...'

A smile was twitching on his lips, and those smoky dark eyes were crinkling in that endearingly familiar way.

'What?' Her voice was defensive, an instinctive reaction to his response. She still read his face so well, almost knew what he was thinking.

'You're still as passionate as ever.' He cleared his throat, as if realising the *faux pas* he had just committed. 'I mean...' His voice trailed off.

Passionate. The word hung in the air between them, conjuring dangerous images of long ago.

Images best forgotten.

Finally he found his voice. 'How on earth do you cope?'

She swallowed hard. 'Red wine helps.' Her words were light and glib, a deliberate attempt to lighten the increasing tension.

'Red wine?'

'Any blood I see, I just imagine it's wine.'

He was really smiling now. 'And does it work?'

'Mostly.'

'And when it doesn't?'

It was Lila's turn to smile now. Rolling her eyes, she pulled a face. 'I just hope for a soft landing.'

'You're not serious?'

'Absolutely. But don't worry,' she added quickly,

'I always get heaps of warning, and I haven't fallen on top of a patient yet—touch wood.'

'Glad to hear it.' There was a long pause as again they pretended to look at the whiteboard. 'How's your mum doing?' His voice was gentle now, wary.

'She's fine. Well, not fine, exactly, but we're managing.'

'That's good.' The silence that followed was deafening. 'Where is she now?'

Lila turned then, the look of contempt on her face clearly apparent. 'At home, Declan, with me—where she belongs.'

'But how…?' His voice was bewildered now. 'It's been eight years. How do you manage? I mean with work and everything?'

'I manage.' She gave him the frostiest of looks. 'That's all you need to know. Now, if you'll excuse me, I need to get on.' But as she went to go his hand reached out and caught her wrist, gently pulling her back.

'Lila,' he said, not letting her go. 'I'm sorry if this makes you uncomfortable—I had no idea that you worked here.'

Though he wasn't holding her tightly, she was achingly aware of the force of his touch. Shrugging him off, Lila picked up a marker pen. 'Well, how would you know? It's not as if we kept in touch…'

'Which was your choice, as I recall.'

Crossing out the name of the patient in cubicle four on the whiteboard, Lila scribbled in the new patient's details. 'I can assure you, Declan, your being here doesn't worry me one bit. We've both got jobs to do. It doesn't mean we have to be the best of friends; we're just colleagues.'

'No, but it would be nice if we could at least be civil. Who knows? With a bit of effort from both sides maybe we *could* be friends again. After all, we had some good times, Lila.'

She hesitated. Friends was the last thing she could ever be with him, but if she betrayed the strength of the emotions that were engulfing her now then surely that would only make things more uncomfortable. Forcing a smile, Lila turned and faced him, dragging her eyes up to meet his. 'Sure—why not?' she said finally, offering her hand. 'Pleased to meet you Dr Haversham.'

'Pleased to meet you, Nurse Bailey. Tell me, would you be interested in catching up for a drink some time?'

Lila's laugh was almost genuine. 'Don't push your luck, Declan. Friends at work is enough to be going on with, I think. Don't you?'

By eleven p.m. the place was full, fit to burst. Not only were there a lot of sick people waiting to be seen and dealt with, but also the pubs were turning out and with them the inevitable fights and arguments that invariably found their way to the emergency department. The staff were all more than used to the organised chaos, and dealt good-humouredly with the constant stream, keeping a careful eye out for any likely sources of trouble.

'I think I've died and gone to heaven,' a young man slurred as the paramedics lifted him over onto a trolley. 'I didn't know nurses were so good-looking.'

Lila rolled her eyes as she pulled on her gloves.

'Fight outside Kerry's pub,' the paramedic reeled off. 'Terry Linton, eighteen years old, multiple lacerations courtesy of a knife; they all appear superficial and his obs have been stable throughout.'

'Thanks, guys. Any more to bring in?'

'But of course.' He gave her a rueful grin, depositing soiled blankets in the linen skip. 'No doubt we'll catch you later.'

'No doubt about it.'

Undressing Terry, Lila ignored his extremely unsubtle advances, concentrating instead on checking each wound carefully. The paramedics were right; they did look superficial—except for one across his left loin. Though small, Lila couldn't assess the depth of the wound, and from the paramedic's description of the knife there was every chance it might have gone deep enough to cause some internal trauma.

'You ever been to Kerry's? You should try it. They have a happy hour every night from five till six, drinks half-price—even those fancy cocktails girls like. I could take you when you get a night off. We'd have a real laugh.'

As Lila placed a wad of Melolin and combine over the leaking wound the tell-tale signs of flashing stars appeared before her eyes.

Why did blood have this effect on her? It was ridiculous that after all these years—after all the study she had done, the sights she had seen—for no reason, completely out of the blue, a small wound such as this could turn her stomach.

'A real laugh,' Lila said dryly, shifting her mind to Terry's attempts at a chat-up. 'I think I might give it a miss, thanks.' Strapping the combine into place, she popped Terry into a gown and quickly recorded a set of obs.

'Need a hand?' Sue's smiling face appeared at the curtain.

'Please. I might move this one over to Resus. Can you give me a hand with the trolley?'

That stopped him in his tracks! 'What are you moving me there for? I'm not dying, am I?'

'No, Terry, I just want to keep a closer eye on you until you've been seen by the doctor.'

'But Resus is where they put the real crook ones.

I've seen it on the telly. You'll be putting those electric shock things on me next.'

Lila grinned. 'You watch too much television, Terry. Look,' she said, slipping an oxygen mask over the young man's face, 'you've got some nasty wounds there. The trouble with knife wounds is that we don't always know how deep they are until they've been explored. I'm just playing it safe by putting you in there for now.'

'So I'm not dying?'

'I certainly hope not—it makes far too much paperwork!' Her humour relaxed Terry, and when she saw him smiling again Lila continued. 'Still, you're not going to be going home tonight. Is there anyone I can ring for you?'

'No way. If my mum finds out she'll kill me. If you think these wounds are bad, just wait till she's finished with me.'

Lila glanced at the casualty card, checking his age with the one the paramedics had given. Terry was eighteen, the decision was his, and, as was common in his age group, Terry had declined to give his telephone number.

'Won't they be expecting you home?'

'No.' He screwed up his nose. 'They'll think I'm staying at me mate's. I mean it. I don't want them told.'

'Up to you,' Lila said. 'But, Terry, if you do become ill—and I'm not saying it's going to happen; I ask this of everyone—can I contact them then?'

Terry looked at her suspiciously.

'I promise I'll only ring them in an emergency.'

'Promise?'

Lila nodded.

'Fair enough.' After relaying the number, Terry sat forward. 'Can you pass me jeans up so I can get some money out? I'll get me mate to fetch me a drink from the machine.'

'Didn't those medical dramas on the television teach you anything?' Lila said good-naturedly. 'Nothing to eat or drink till the doctor's seen you.'

Declan was tied up, so it was left to the intern, Diana Pool, to assess Terry.

'They all seem pretty superficial, though I see what you mean about the one to his loin. I'd better refer him to the surgeons. I know Mr Hinkley doesn't like knife wounds to be sutured down in the department.'

'Good call,' Lila agreed. Mr Hinkley was senior consultant of the emergency department and, though not the most exciting of personalities, he was a diligent and respected boss.

The trouble was that Jez, the surgical resident, though thorough in his examination, was less than impressed with the referral.

'They're fairly minor injuries. I'm happy for him to be stitched up and discharged.'

'Fair enough. If you're happy then so am I.' Diana accepted back the casualty card Jez had hastily scribbled on.

'Sorry, guys.' Lila, anticipating trouble, had been discreetly hovering. 'He's a surgical patient now—it's not up to Diana to stitch him.'

Jez pursed his lips. He was young and good-looking, and also far too used to getting his own way—only not when Lila was on duty. 'Fine,' he snapped. 'If that's the way you want to play it then I'll do it myself, but can I at least have a nurse to help in the operating theatre?'

Lila's voice remained calm, friendly even, but there was no mistaking the seriousness of her tone. 'I'm afraid not, Jez. You know as well as I do that surgical patients can't be stitched down in Emergency. Our operating room's only designed for superficial wounds.'

'Which these are.'

'Not according to Mr Hinkley: "A stab wound can only be considered superficial when the wound has been thoroughly explored." He'll either have to go to the main theatre or be stitched up on the ward, if your boss agrees. It's the department's policy.'

'Since when were you such a stickler for policy?' Declan's friendly tones as he made his way over broke the rather tense atmosphere that had developed.

'When the policy concerned is in the best interests of a patient then I'm a stickler.' Lila turned defiantly from Jez to Declan. 'I have a young man with multiple lacerations. One in particular looks deep—'

'It isn't,' Jez broke in. 'Look, I'm happy for him to be stitched up, I've even offered to do it myself, but the nurse here insists he goes up to Theatre or at least a ward. Considering that the rest of the surgical team are stuck in Theatre, it could be hours until he's seen.' He threw a withering look at Lila. 'And we all know the department's *policy* about patient waiting times.'

Declan grinned as Lila gritted her teeth. 'So it's stalemate?'

'It would seem so.' Lila found she was holding her breath. She knew she was right, and that Mr Hinkley and even Hester, come to that, would support her on this. But that wasn't what was worrying her. Declan's take on this mattered, and not just in a medical sense. If they were going to work together effectively as a team, if they were going to cast aside their differences in the name of peace, she needed his support here.

Her personal feelings, her innermost thoughts, didn't apply—at least, she tried not to let them.

'Can I see the casualty card?'

Jez handed it over, watching as Declan flicked through the notes.

'You're a braver man than me!' Declan looked up. 'I personally wouldn't like to stand up in court and explain my findings based on these notes.'

'He has superficial wounds,' Jez insisted, though rather less forcibly. Declan was, after all, far more senior than him.

'Appears to have,' Declan said, his face suddenly serious. 'As Lila pointed out, until the wounds are thoroughly explored by a senior doctor they cannot be called superficial. Now, I suggest you get your registrar down here, and if he doesn't want to take the patient to Theatre I'll repeat my argument to him. And one other thing,' he said as he handed back the casualty card to a fuming Jez, 'I'd try listening to the nursing staff a bit more if I were you. They can make your life one hell of a lot easier.'

As Jez flounced off to the telephone Lila realised a thank-you might be in order. But that didn't stop it sticking in her throat. 'Thanks for that.'

'No worries. I meant what I said. The last thing a doctor needs is the emergency nurses offside, particularly the night team. If Jez doesn't realise that then it's time he learnt. Now, if there are any problems with the reg, be sure and let me know. How are Terry's obs?'

'Stable.'

'Good.'

She knew she should go now—after all there were a hundred and one things that needed to be done—but for some reason Lila found her legs wouldn't move.

'I've just seen a Vera Hamilton. From the pile of notes outside her cubicle I assume she's a regular?'

Lila nodded. 'We all know Vera. What's wrong tonight? Her leg ulcer?'

'So she says. Frankly, I can't see much to write home about.'

Lila laughed. 'Vera's a manic depressive. She works her way back to us about once a month under various guises, and her "leg ulcer" is the most common excuse.'

'She just needs a dry dressing. I offered to do it, but she said you normally took care of her.'

'No worries. I'll get around to her when I can.'

The conversation was over, or at least it should have been, but he still stood there.

And to her utter surprise it was she herself who resurrected it. 'Do you fancy a curry?'

'Lila!' Declan's face broke into a grin. 'I'll have to defend you more often. A couple of hours ago you wouldn't even consider a drink, now you're asking me out for dinner.'

'In your dreams.' Lila grinned. 'The staff have a whip-round about now and ring for a take-away.

Tonight is curry night.' She couldn't be certain, but she was almost sure a hint of a blush crept over his face as he reached for his wallet.

'How much?'

'That should do it.' Cheekily she grabbed a ten-dollar note from his hands. 'And we don't complicate things by taking individual orders. 'Chicken Jalfrezi with saffron rice and Kashmiri naan are the go tonight.'

'Sounds great. When do we get to eat?'

'When you get rid of all the patients.'

Whether the delicious fragrance of curry proved an incentive, or whether it was merely the fact that Declan was a good worker, by three a.m. most of the patients had been moved up to the wards or stitched and sent home. A couple of patients remained, awaiting X-rays and bloods, and two or three of the city's homeless slept soundly on trolleys.

'I don't know what it is about you,' Sue said, laughing as she tucked a blanket around Henry, one of their regular tramps, 'but all the down-and-outs seem to congregate here the nights you're on. Could it have something to do with the breakfast you order them from the kitchen?'

Lila shrugged. 'They don't do any harm. I mean, they're happy to wait in the waiting room until the place is quieter, and they all have ulcers and the like that do need to be treated. A few hours' sleep on a warm trolley and breakfast is hardly a big deal.'

'It would be if the Horse found out.'

'I'll deal with that when it happens. Come on, Sue, I'm starving.'

The curry was set up in the small relatives' room at the entrance to the department. The position was ideal for confused and anxious relatives while their loved one was whizzed on to Resus. During quiet times it served also as an extra staffroom for the night crew. From here they had a full view of any new patients, could hear the tyre screeches of a car pulling up, and if the need arose any curries or pizzas were cleared away more hastily than if one's mother-in-law had just descended for a surprise visit.

Peeling the cardboard lids off the foil containers, Lila managed a grimace at the rather unkempt plates.

'Get your hands off me, you horrible man!' Vera's far from dulcet tones carried the length and breadth of the department.

'I think Declan just tried to dress Vera's ulcer.' Lila laughed.

'You never let him go without warning him about Vera?' Sue choked. 'The poor guy! What did he ever do to you?'

Spooning the rice onto plates, Lila kept her face hidden from Sue's scrutiny.

'He did plenty,' Lila muttered, more to herself than to Sue. 'He did plenty.'

'She loves me really.' Declan's face appeared round the door and Lila flushed unbecomingly. How much had he heard?

She stopped furiously spooning curry as she realised one plate was receiving rather more than its fair share of chicken Jalfrezi.

'The only person Vera loves is Lila,' Sue said matter-of-factly, and with relief Lila realised Declan's comments had been purely about the patient.

'I told you I'd get round to her,' Lila said tartly, handing Declan an overloaded plate.

'Four hours ago,' he said pointedly. 'Look, I know you've been busy, and that her leg ulcer's not serious, but it just seemed a shame that she was still waiting. I was only trying to help.'

'Vera's happy to wait,' she explained with a cheeky grin. 'More than happy. Normally I get around to her about six a.m.—about the time early breakfasts are served. The last thing she wants is to be seen and discharged.'

'Why didn't you tell me that?' He gave a wry laugh. 'But then that would have spoiled your fun, wouldn't it?'

Lila scuffed at the floor with her foot. Hell, it had only been a bit of fun—so why was she suddenly feeling so guilty?

'New boy's tease,' she said finally, knowing how hollow her words sounded.

Picking up his supper, he gave her a bemused look. 'Well, I'm glad you enjoyed the cabaret.'

'That,' said Declan scraping his plate, 'would have to be the best curry I've had in years. Is it always as busy as this here?'

'Always,' Lila said truthfully. 'You wait for the weekend. Where were you working before?'

'In a lovely county hospital in bonny Scotland. Mind you, I was in London before then—and that was an eye-opener, I can assure you.'

Lila deliberately didn't look impressed. 'I remember visiting an emergency room in New York when I was a flight attendant—it made here look like a picnic in the park.'

'New York's busy,' Declan agreed. 'Or at least it was when I was there. But you want to see the emergency rooms in Chicago—they're constantly full-on.'

Lila picked up the last of the naan bread. 'I'm not going to win, am I? So what brought you back to good old Melbourne?'

He was saved from answering as Jez appeared at the door, carrying flowers.

'Lila, I come in peace.' Handing her the bouquet, Jez gave her an embarrassed smile. 'I nicked them from Admin on my way back from Theatre.'

'How's Terry?' Lila asked, accepting the rather wilted offering.

'Bled out on the way up to Theatre—a nasty wound to his kidney. Thankfully we were able to repair it. He's in Recovery now.'

'Then it's just as well he wasn't stitched and sent home.' Lila couldn't resist stating the obvious, but she was smiling.

'Lesson well and truly learnt,' Jez said seriously, and, ignoring the crowd of staff gathered, carried on talking to Lila, undaunted by his audience. 'I think I owe you a proper thank-you. How about dinner some time?'

The sniggers from Sue and Lucy didn't go unnoticed.

'Thanks, Jez, but it might get a bit expensive. I mean, there's Declan and Diana to thank as well. The flowers will do nicely.'

As he left, Lila returned to her seat amid the howls of her colleagues. 'How do you do it, Lila? Gorgeous men dropping at your feet and you just kick them away.'

The only one not joining in with the laughter was Declan. Suddenly his empty plate was being examined thoroughly.

'Oh, I don't know,' Lila said softly. 'Years of practice, I guess. I mean, it starts off with meals and flowers, but we all know how it ends up.'

Declan looked up, catching her eye as he did so. This time she held his gaze, her words directed at him alone. 'And I'm never going to be let down again.'

CHAPTER TWO

'Hi, Lila, how was your night?'

'Pretty busy.' Lila kissed her aunt, Shirley, on the cheek. 'How has Mum been?'

'The same. We'll have a cuppa and then we'll give her a bath.' Shirley filled the kettle, as she did every morning when Lila arrived home, but there was something wooden about her movements, an awkwardness that didn't go undetected. 'Lila, I need to talk to you about something.'

Lila felt her heart plummet. She had known this day was coming, and in the last few weeks had sensed it was even more imminent. Sitting at the kitchen table, she tried for a futile moment to imagine she'd somehow misread the signs. But as Shirley joined her, unable to meet her eyes, Lila knew the news she had been dreading was about to be delivered.

'Your uncle Ted has been offered early retirement,' Shirley said finally.

Ted was a security officer and worked the same shifts as Lila. It worked well, or at least it had until now... While Ted worked Shirley looked after

Elizabeth, and when Ted was off Lila took over, allowing Ted and Shirley to live their lives.

'He wants to take it, Lila. I didn't want to worry you with our problems but Ted has been having a few health issues of his own. Nothing to worry about,' she quickly reassured her as she saw the look of concern flash over Lila's face. 'Just a couple of men's issues. He'd be so embarrassed if he knew I was discussing it with you. The thing is, Ted deserves his retirement. He's worked so hard. We want to be able to go away, have holidays. We always dreamed of taking the combo van and travelling around Australia...' Shirley dabbed at her eyes with a tissue. 'I feel so torn. Elizabeth's my sister. I'd do anything to help her. But Ted's my husband, and he's been a good one. How many men would take in their sister-in-law and niece? I'm sorry,' she said quickly, 'I didn't mean it to come out like that.'

'I know,' Lila said softly, taking her aunt's hand from across the table to show that no offence had been taken. 'You and Ted have been marvellous.'

They had been. Almost as soon as Elizabeth had been diagnosed, Shirley, realising the impossibility of the situation, had suggested that both Lila and Elizabeth move in with her and Ted to share the burden. Shirley was an eccentric, to say the least, and with no children of their own, opening their house the way they had, it had been a huge upheaval. Yet they had borne it all cheerfully, never once grumbling about how their lives had been turned around by Elizabeth's illness.

But now it was time for change.

'I know you don't want her to go into a home. But, Lila, your mum…' She struggled for the words to describe the shell that remained of what had once been an elegant, eloquent woman. 'Your mum wouldn't know any different.'

'But *I'd* know. Mum would hate the—'

'She'd hate the fact you've given up your life to look after her,' Shirley interrupted. 'She'd hate the fact you work so hard and then come home at the end of a long night just to start all over again. Hate the fact you hardly ever go out.'

Lila searched for an answer. The last thing she wanted to do was make this horrible situation worse for Shirley, to make her feel guilty for saying the words most people would have said years ago. But a home…

'Now, Ted's retirement isn't going to happen for a couple of months yet. We don't have to make any decision today, Lila, but we are going to have to soon.' She smiled through her tears at her niece. 'I'm not definitely saying your mum has to go into a home; I'm saying I can't be here as much to help. My back is starting to hurt—lifting her, turning her.

I just don't see an end to it. You understand where I'm coming from, don't you, Lila?'

Lila made her way around the table to hug her aunt as she spoke. 'Of course I do.' She swallowed back her own tears. 'And I promise I'll come up with something.'

'I know you will, pet. What worries me is *what* you'll come up with. You're thirty-one years old now, Lila—you can't let your life slip by like this. It's not good for any of us, least of all your mother. Look, I've probably said too much for one day already. Why don't you head off to bed, darling, try and get some sleep?'

Lila nodded, but as she reached the door she turned. 'Shirley, there's some forms I need to drop off at the hospital before five. Would you be able to watch Mum for me?'

'Of course, darling.'

Alone in her room, Lila pulled the application forms out of her bag. It had never really entered her head to apply, but Hester's words had made the chance of promotion a real possibility. Now, with Shirley's bombshell... Closing her eyes, Lila tried to search for answers. How could she possibly afford a caregiver to stay with Elizabeth while she went out to work? It would be more cost effective to go on the dole and nurse her mum full time herself.

But... She felt a tinge of panic hit. How could she

give up her job? OK, she wasn't the best nurse in the world, and she moaned like everyone else about the shortages and workload, but she truly loved her job—loved the people, loved the escape work gave her from her everyday problems. How could she even begin to think about giving it up?

Clicking her pen open, she started to work her way through the endless forms. If she was going to have to employ someone to help her look after her mother, a decent wage was more important now than ever.

If there was any consolation to be had from the day's events, it was that Lila didn't have time to dwell on Declan's return. Any other time it would have completely overwhelmed her, but not today. Today was a day for filling out forms, working out figures, planning a future—not dwelling on the past, imagining days long since gone, a time when Declan had been beside her.

A time when life had been easy.

Hester took the forms without a word, which made Lila's journey to the hospital somewhat of an anti-climax. Only when she returned home and fed Elizabeth her supper, then settled her into bed for the night, did Lila's stomach suddenly tighten at the thought of seeing Declan again tonight.

Maybe she did tie up her hair more neatly and apply her make-up just a little bit more carefully, but it was more a matter of personal pride than vanity. She certainly wasn't going to allow Declan to think even for a minute that she had let herself go.

That was a joke. Eyeing her reflection in the mirror, Lila paused a moment. Her naturally thick blonde hair was as glossy as ever, her figure still trim. But the sparkle in her blue eyes was long since gone, and a quick slick of mascara and a neutral lipstick replaced the immaculate glossy make-up of yesteryear.

'Well, what did you expect?' Lila scolded herself. 'You're not a flight attendant now.' It had been easy to look stunning then, with cheap access to the world's best cosmetics, advice from the airline's stylists, her nails and hair done weekly. And, Lila thought reluctantly, she was eight years older now—eight long years. Of course her skin wasn't going to be quite as clear. She was the wrong side of thirty now, not some twenty-something beauty.

Poking her tongue out at her reflection, Lila caught sight of the clock on her dressing-table. With a yelp of dismay she pulled on her shoes and grabbed her bag, just stopping to give her mother and Shirley a quick kiss before she torpedoed out of the front door and into her car.

So much for making a good impression on Hester!

For once the department was quiet, with just a few patients waiting to be seen by various specialists or awaiting their turn for X-rays. As soon as the day staff had gone Lila pulled the kettle round to the nurses' station.

'Might as well get our caffeine levels up while we've got the chance.' She grinned.

'Good idea.' Yvonne Selles walked over. 'It's Lila, isn't it?'

'That's right. How can I help you, Dr Selles? Apart from the coffee, I mean?'

'Please, call me Yvonne. I'm expecting a direct admission from a nursing home. I wasn't quite sure of the procedure as my ward is full, so I've asked the ambulance to bring her directly to Emergency. I hope that's all right.'

'That's fine. Thanks for letting us know. What's wrong with the patient?'

'Pressure sores, along with dehydration. I shouldn't have accepted her really, as I haven't got any beds left, but according to the GP she's in a bit of a mess and I could hardly refuse to take her. Her GP was pretty upset the home didn't call him out a lot sooner. Some of these nursing homes need to take a good long look at themselves. It seems more about profit than people these days. Sorry.' Yvonne gave a thin smile. 'I'll get off my soapbox now. It just gets to me sometimes.'

'I know,' Lila said softly, swallowing a lump in

her own throat. 'It gets to me, too. Anyway—' she deliberately brightened her voice '—there's a couple of free beds on the medical ward. If you admit the patient to Med 1 you can transfer her over to the Acute Geriatric Unit tomorrow.'

'Looking for some action, Yvonne?' Grinning, Declan joined the group.

In an instant Lila felt as if her senses had been put on high alert. She could almost feel the breeze from him as he walked over.

'He thinks only staff in Emergency do any work.' Yvonne grinned. 'Just because my patients are old, it doesn't mean they're not sick,' she scolded lightly. 'I still have to use my brain.'

Lila jumped down from her stool as Harry, the porter, wheeled a patient back from X-Ray. 'Declan, would you mind having a quick look at these? Diana thinks it may be pneumonia and he'll probably need to be referred on.'

'Sure.'

With an easy smile he took the X-rays from Harry and made his way over to the viewing box.

'Phew,' Yvonne said. 'It's a different place here at night.'

'We're not normally this quiet,' Sue said almost defensively.

'I didn't mean that.' Yvonne smiled. 'It's just so much more relaxed and friendly. I was down here this afternoon and the unit manager nearly had a fit because I brought my coffee round the front.'

'That'd be right,' Lila groaned.

'So how come it's so different down here at night?'

'Different staff,' Lila said, climbing back onto the high stool. 'Night staff on the whole are a lot nicer—in my opinion, of course. We're not all pulled into the politics of days, fighting over any interesting patients, trying to look busy when it's quiet.' She laughed. 'Now, who's up on their soapbox?'

'And what does Hester have to say about all this?' Yvonne gestured to the tray overloaded with cups and cakes and biscuits.

'Plenty,' Lila admitted. 'But I've told her that when she provides enough staff so that we can have our full breaks I'll put away the running buffet, but until then it stays. Speaking of which, I'm going to have a huge slice of cake—do you fancy a piece?'

'Just a small one, and then I'd better get on and do some work.'

'Where were you before you worked here?' Lila asked, plunging a knife into a vast walnut cake.

'Home—Scotland,' Yvonne added.

'So what brings you to Melbourne?'

Yvonne shrugged. 'I just fancied a change, a few personal reasons.'

'Declan was saying he worked in Scotland for a

while,' Sue commented as the knife Lila was holding froze in the cake.

'He's one of the personal reasons,' Yvonne said lightly.

'You worked with him there.' Suddenly Lila's voice was strangely high.

'A bit more than that,' Yvonne admitted, and Lila saw she was blushing.

'So you're an item?' Sue pushed happily, delighted to be the first with the gossip.

'Well, we *are* living together,' Yvonne admitted, blushing ever deeper as she did so. 'So, yes, I guess we are.'

The knife was working rapidly now, slicing the cake with lightning speed. It had never even entered her head. Not for a single second. Even with Yvonne's accent, even when Declan had mentioned he'd worked in Scotland, even the fact they'd started on the same day. Not once had it occurred to Lila that they might be together.

There just didn't seem to be anything between them. OK, so she'd hardly seen them together, just at Yvonne's lecture and for a couple of minutes this evening, but there was nothing that had indicated to Lila they were a couple. No stolen glances, no sexual tension, nothing. Yes, they were at work. And, yes, you didn't have to be constantly touching to be a couple, but surely there would have been some vibe?

Surely. Her mind whizzed back eight years. They could have been on the other side of the room yet there had always been an energy between them—a constant awareness that had permeated the room.

She wasn't still hung up on Declan—it was over, over, over.

It just seemed so unfair, that was all. His life had moved on, ever onwards, while she herself seemed frozen where he'd left her. And not even there, apart from her wardrobe perhaps. Eight years ago she had been stunning, had had a great social life and a glamorous job. Eight years, five extra kilos and no social life later, that's where Declan had found her.

'Are you still here?' Declan grinned at Yvonne.

The same way he grinned at everyone, everyone except her.

'Still here. One more patient to admit and then I'll head off home, though I think I might wait for her to arrive in the doctors' mess and have a doze while I'm waiting. I don't suppose you picked up milk, like I asked?'

Yvonne glanced over at Lila, an almost imperceptible flash of triumph in her eyes. She knows about us, Lila realised, and she's making sure I know that they're together now.

'Of course I didn't,' Declan answered cheerfully, completely oblivious to the sudden tension in the tiny annex. 'I've rung Chest Med, Lila,' he said, changing the subject. 'They want the patient sent straight up to the ward and they'll clerk him there.'

'I'll go,' Sue said, swinging down from the work bench.

But Yvonne hadn't finished turning the knife. 'Anything else you want me to pick up from the all-night store, Declan—anything you fancy?'

Declan laughed 'Plenty, but let's just leave it at milk for now, huh?'

Once Yvonne had gone Declan helped himself to a huge piece of cake. 'Who made this?'

'Lila,' Sue said as she picked up the patients' files and headed off to the ward.

'Really?' Declan took a tentative bite and grabbed his throat. 'Put out a crash call, I've been poisoned.'

'Very funny,' Lila said, suddenly finding her tongue. 'But, then, everything always was a joke to you.'

'What's that supposed to mean?' Declan asked, his voice suddenly serious.

'You know full well.'

'No, Lila, I don't. What have I done now?'

She shot him a look. 'You mean apart from strolling back into my life and expecting us to be *friends*?'

'Yes, Lila.' His voice was deep and his eyes searched hers. 'Yes, Lila,' he repeated. 'Apart from that.'

What could she say? That the news he was living

with Yvonne had devastated her? That, though she hadn't even realised it, she had somehow harboured a hope that maybe, just maybe there might have been a chance for them?

Of course not. She tore her eyes away. Lying was hard enough without looking at him. 'I think I made a mistake yesterday,' she replied finally, 'when I said we could be friends. There's too much water under the bridge.'

She turned to go, but for the second time in as many days he caught her arm again, stopping her from leaving, forcing her not to leave the conversation there.

'If anyone should be hurt about the water under the bridge, Lila, it's me.'

'What?' Unable to believe her ears, she shot him a furious look. 'You think you were the one that got hurt?'

'You finished it, Lila.'

'I'm back. Anyone else to go up?' Sue barged in, oblivious to the conversation that was taking place.

'Sue, I just need a word with Lila,' Declan said quickly.

'That won't be necessary, doctor.' Pointedly Lila pulled her arm away.

'No, you two go right ahead,' Sue said brightly, ignoring Lila's desperate eye signals. 'I'll buzz if things pick up out here.'

They ended up in Hester's office, Lila's cheeks burning with anger and the strangest awareness at finding herself finally alone with him. As Declan closed the door he turned slowly, his face serious. Suddenly he looked older, so much older than the carefree young man she had once known.

'You finished with me,' he said, as if the last couple of minutes had never happened. 'You were the one who ended two years with a single phone call. Who packed up and moved without leaving a forwarding address. Hell, I've still got a box of records and clothes you left at my place, make-up and jewellery you left on my dressing-table which you never came back for.' His voice was rising now, and Lila was stunned to hear the pain behind it. 'And you think you're the one that got hurt?'

Lila shook her head angrily. 'You sound like you don't know why I went, Declan. You sound as if you truly believe you did nothing wrong.'

'What, Lila? What did I do to merit that? I knew you were upset about your mother. I knew you'd had a shock, but to just vanish like that...'

She had never once looked at this from his point of view, too full of anger and hurt to have believed there had been another side to this painful story. But he deserved to be hurt, Lila reminded herself, a steely resolve returning. He deserved it.

'You laughed at me,' she rasped, years of pain

welling to the surface. 'I needed you to be there for me and you laughed.'

Declan's face was incredulous. She watched the colour drain from his cheeks as he listened to her words.

'Lila.' He shook his head, bewildered. 'I never laughed at you, never.'

'When I said I wanted to do nursing,' she reminded him, the memory of that day seared into her brain with aching clarity.

'But I wasn't laughing at you. I was confused, trying to make you see sense. Lila, you hated blood, hated anything like that. Fair play to you, you've gone on and done it and from what I can see you're a fabulous nurse. But back then... Lila, we were so young, so carefree, surely you can see why I laughed. I laughed at the idea, never you.

'I'd have been there for you. I'd have helped—I truly would have. Hell, Lila, the moment you walked out I got all my books out, tried to find out more about Alzheimer's to see if there were any new treatments, any drugs or advances. It never even entered my head you weren't coming back to me.'

Lila shook her head, unable to take Declan's slant on things, refusing any attempt at an explanation. What she expected next from Declan she truly didn't know, a further attempt to justify the past perhaps, a plea for understanding, an apology perhaps. Certainly not what did come next.

'You're telling me that you threw it all away on the basis of a misplaced laugh?'

Lila looked up sharply at him, her blue eyes meeting his steely grey ones. Not a hint of the carefree charmer she'd known so well looked back at her. No lazy smile, no crinkle as his eyes met hers now. Just the cold steel of his stare.

'You hurt me,' she intoned.

For the longest time he stared, bewilderment clouding his eyes for an instant. But only for an instant, the ice soon returning.

'What the hell do you think you did to me, then?' And turning, he left her standing there.

Suddenly her entire perspective of that fateful day had shifted. That bitter argument had formed the basis for a burning and later simmering anger, an anger that had stayed with her for eight long years. An anger that had kept the pain of her loss at bay.

For she had lost so much on that day—her partner, her lover, her best friend.

As the horror truly dawned, Lila put a shaking hand up to her lips.

Had she been so blind that she had let everything go? Let everything go for nothing?

CHAPTER THREE

'OH, COME on, Lila, even if you just come for an hour.'

Lila shook her head. 'Sorry, Sue, I really can't.'

'But why not?' Sue insisted. 'You don't have to buy anything, it's more just an excuse to have a glass of wine and a bit of a giggle.'

A glass of wine and a bit of a giggle sounded pretty tempting, but the logistics of going to Sue's lingerie party simply weren't worth it. Lila hated dumping on Shirley. Particularly on a Saturday night and even more so now.

Somehow, and probably with no good reason, she didn't want Shirley to feel even more tied to her sister. Didn't want to add any more fuel to the fire.

'Give me a copy of the brochure,' Lila suggested. 'I'll buy something.'

Handing over a brochure, Sue gave Lila a worried look. 'I don't want you there just to buy something.'

'I know,' Lila assured her, acutely aware that Declan had just joined them at the nurses' station.

'So why can't you come?'

Lila shrugged dismissively.

'You never seem to go out...'

Lila shot Sue a look that told her to be quiet, but, unperturbed, Sue continued relentlessly. 'There's the emergency department ball in a couple of weeks. I bet you don't go to that either.'

Declan seemed to be concentrating hard on the notes he was writing, but Lila was positive he was listening.

'I might,' Lila said lightly.

'But that's what you always say, and then you end up not going. Come on, Lila, if you can't come to my lingerie party at least come to the ball. I'm not taking no for an answer. We single girls need to stick together, and anyway it will be fun.'

'What, seeing the Horse in a new blanket?'

Sue grinned. 'Can I put your name down, then? Everyone will be rapt if you finally make it to something.'

Lila took a deep breath. Sue had a point. She rarely attended work functions, and the truth was that her low social profile was starting to be noticed.

'OK, OK, I'll come,' Lila said finally, to keep Sue quiet in front of Declan.

'When you've finished arranging your social schedule, there's a patient I'd like a hand with, Nurse.' Declan's animosity didn't go unnoticed.

It had been two weeks since their confrontation in Hester's office. Two long weeks where they had studiously avoided each other or, when forced to, had spoken *almost* politely.

At work she coped, or at least appeared to. Not quite the consummate professional—the chance of a promotion wasn't that inviting. But she worked diligently, determined that Declan shouldn't see how hurt she was, how he had overturned her world just by coming back.

How devastated she was that he was seeing Yvonne.

'Ellen Whiting, eighty-four year old. She's been admitted from a nursing home with fever for investigation. I need you to help me sit her up so that I can listen to her chest.'

'Fine,' Lila replied crisply, though her heart sank. It had been hard enough putting on a façade of friendliness, but even that had been so much easier than this obvious animosity.

All that was put aside, though, as they entered the cubicle to examine the patient. Ellen Whiting was a tiny, frail lady, barely conscious.

'Mrs Whiting, I'm Dr Declan Haversham and I'm going to examine you and see if we can't make you a bit more comfortable.'

The genuine tenderness in his voice, the gentle way he examined the frail lady came as a surprise to Lila. She had never for a moment expected him to be brusque, but the compassion he showed the elderly woman as he gently probed her abdomen and listened to her chest was another painful glimpse of the man she had lost.

'Could you help me to lift her forward so that I can listen to the back of her chest?'

Between them they gently sat Ellen forward and Lila pulled up her nightgown to enable Declan to listen with his stethoscope.

'She'll need a chest X-ray,' he said once he had finished listening. 'I'm going to put in an IV and get some fluids started. And then take some bloods and we'll get some antibiotics going.'

He scribbled his orders on the casualty card and handed it to Lila without looking up.

'I'll get the IV trolley,' Lila suggested helpfully, but Declan shook his head.

'No problem. I can manage. If you can just get the antibiotics drawn up, that would be good.'

Standing at the drug cupboard, she knew he was near before she saw him.

'Have you seen my tourniquet?' Declan asked finally, when it was obvious he couldn't find it anywhere.

'No. Here, use mine.' But as she pulled it out of her pocket Declan shook his head.

'It's all right, it must be around somewhere.'

Lila pursed her lips. 'Would you like me to pull the drugs up in another room while you look?'

His brow furrowed at the sarcasm in her voice. 'Sorry? What are you going on about?'

'I can pull the drugs up elsewhere if it makes you so uncomfortable—being in the same room as me, I mean.'

Declan gave a weary sigh. 'I have no idea what you're talking about, Lila.'

'Oh, I think you do, Dr Haversham. Just remember, while you're spending so much time trying to avoid me, it was you that suggested we be friends, at least at work. You were the one who said you didn't want me feeling uncomfortable.'

'And are you?'

Lila took a deep breath. 'Yes,' she admitted. 'And it's not only me. All the staff know there's an atmosphere, they have no idea why.'

Declan shrugged, looking up as she caught her breath in irritation. 'What have I done wrong now?'

'I'd forgotten how much that irritated me. The way you shrug things off, the way you just dismiss what I'm saying.'

'Poor Lila,' he said slowly. 'Poor, hard-done-by Lila. I've treated you so badly, haven't I?'

Suddenly the keys in her hand came under close scrutiny as she avoided his searing gaze.

'Not only did I laugh at the wrong moment eight years ago, but I had the audacity to accept a promotion in my home town without checking whether you'd had a career change and might possibly be on the staff. I'm just so thoughtless sometimes.'

His sarcasm bit through her.

'And then,' he continued, 'when I try to discuss things with you, check things are all right with you, like a fool I believe you when you say things are fine, that we'll put the past behind us and be friends. Now, Lila, if my memory serves me correctly, you then suddenly decided that, no, we can't be friends any more, so, like an idiot, I try not to exacerbate things by backing off a bit. Hell, I'm such a bastard sometimes.'

Holding the syringe of antibiotics in front of her eyes, she flicked the tiny air bubbles out with her fingers, biting back tears.

'Have you finished?'

'Oh, I'm finished all right,' he said wearily. 'I'm finished trying to work out what makes you tick, Lila. Finished trying to be nice.

'And in case you were hoping this job might be a stop-gap, you couldn't be more wrong. I'm through with travelling and I intend to stay around a while, so you'd better get used to having me around.'

He made to go then stopped suddenly. 'One final thing. I wasn't going to the ball this Saturday, even though I'm expected to go. Even though it's the first social occasion since I've been here and it could only help me to settle in. The nice guy that I am had decided as you were going I'd make things easier on both of us and stay away. But seeing as the gloves are off now, when you put your name down on the list, do me a favour and add mine.

'And guess what?' he added nastily. He took the syringe of antibiotics from her and, checking the vial, gave her a wintry smile. 'I might even ask the charming Nurse Bailey for a dance.'

CHAPTER FOUR

'YOU'RE positive you don't mind?' Lila checked with Shirley for the umpteenth time, half wishing for a last-minute reprieve.

'Of course I don't mind. Ted's just been to the video shop and hired a couple of movies.' She opened the carrier bag on the kitchen table and giggled. 'I don't know what's got into him all of a sudden—romantic films, he's bought a bottle of wine for tonight and a box of my favourite chocolates—so don't you even think about coming home early. Who knows what you might find!'

That was just a tad too much information for Lila's liking but she managed a grin. 'It's been so long since I've been out I'll probably turn into a pumpkin if I stay out past midnight.'

They were sitting in the kitchen, face packs on and heated rollers in as they painted each other's nails.

'Rubbish. Anyway, it will do you the world of good. You used to love going out. What are you going to wear?'

'If only I knew!'

'But you've got loads of gorgeous dresses in your wardrobe.'

Lila rolled her eyes. 'If you like taffeta.'

'What about that lovely black dress, the one you wore for my silver wedding anniversary? You can't tell me that's gone out of fashion. I can remember your mother telling me how much you paid for it. With that price tag surely "timeless elegance" should stand for something?'

'I don't even know where it is,' Lila answered, trying to remember what it even looked like. When Shirley and Ted had celebrated their silver wedding Lila hadn't thought twice about blowing a week's wages on the best dress. Stopovers in New York had been spent admiring the gorgeous dresses in the best fashion houses. She hadn't been rich but with a good wage and no responsibilities it had been all too easy to justify the expense.

'It's in a suitcase above your mum's wardrobe.'

It was, too. Impossibly skimpy, and not black— more a dark charcoal grey—a silk slip covered with grey chiffon and the scantiest straps holding it up.

'I'll never get into it,' Lila gasped as she ripped the plastic dry-cleaner's bag open.

But she did. Admittedly there was absolutely no way she could eat all night and there could be a dangerous moment if one of the straps gave way, but with her blonde hair pinned up and her make-up carefully applied for the first time in years Lila felt a shimmer of excitement when she looked in the mirror.

'You look gorgeous,' Shirley enthused. 'Stunning. You have to show your mum.'

Gently opening the bedroom door, Lila made her way into the bedroom. The radio was playing gently, the electric aromatherapy lantern lending a delicate-jasmine fragrance. Elizabeth lay on the bed, her tiny frame supported by a mountain of pillows, her unseeing eyes not moving as Lila entered.

'I'm going out tonight, Mum. I just thought I'd show you my dress.' Sitting on the bed, she took her mother's hand in her own. 'I wore it to Ted and Shirley's silver wedding, remember?'

She ran her mother's hand against the fabric. 'You told me off when you found the receipt then boasted to everyone there how much I'd spent.' Lila laughed but there was a catch in it as her mother just lay there.

Was she remembering? Did anything reach her? As they sat there, the music playing in the background, it was Lila who remembered that night. How Declan had been there with her, chatting and laughing with everyone, dancing the embarrassing dances that seemed mandatory on these nights as if it were the best party he had ever been to. He'd loved this dress, too.

Lila closed her eyes as the memories started to

flood in. Memories that she'd pushed away for so long.

The giggles as he'd tried to locate the zip hidden at the side within the seam. Gently pulling it down, her gasp as his warm hands had slipped inside the flimsy fabric, her warm breast waiting, tingling for his touch, the admiration in his eyes as the fabric had fluttered down to her slender ankles...

Lila arrived fashionably late, of course. She didn't bother her colleagues with the details, but by the time Elizabeth had been washed and changed and washed and changed again the meal was already starting.

'I thought you weren't coming!'

'I said I'd be here, didn't I?' Lila grinned slipping into her seat as her colleagues nodded and waved at her.

'Have I missed anything?' she asked as the waiter filled her glass.

'Well,' Sue whispered loudly, 'The Horse has a slick of blue eye shadow on and has knocked up the most amazing tartan dress from one of Trigger's old blankets, and Mr Hinkley has for once in his life added a splash of whisky to his water, but apart from that, no, you didn't miss much.'

Lila was about to execute a smart reply but Declan's arrival from the bar, depositing his drinks directly in front of her, seemed to find Lila suddenly tongue-tied.

He seemed to start for an instant when he saw her sitting there, his gaze flicking over her. As a deep blush swept over her Lila was grateful for the dimmed lights. Surely he didn't remember the dress, remember that night…

'Actually—' Sue's voice was quieter now and she spoke from behind her menu '—Yvonne is knocking it back like it's going out of fashion. I don't think Declan's too impressed.'

Lila looked over. Yvonne did indeed have that dangerous glint in her eye as she tipped her wine into the glass Declan had brought over. She was dressed to kill; crushed red velvet draped her figure, her bust spilling out over the top. She was all over him, embarrassingly so, and Declan looked far from impressed, pulling his hand away when she grabbed it, ducking his face away as she moved in to whisper to him.

'Maybe they had a row before they came out,' Lila suggested.

'I don't know about that,' Sue said dramatically, 'but I can guarantee there'll be one hell of a row when they get home.'

The food was delicious, or at least everyone said it was, but for Lila the food was the last thing on her mind. Declan was close, so close. Sitting directly opposite her, she couldn't help but see him.

She could feel him watching her also, though she tried to ignore him. Tried to concentrate on what her friends were saying, to laugh at their jokes, to hopefully look like she was having some fun.

The waiter came round with the main course, depositing the alternate meals as the table surveyed what they had been given.

'Chicken or beef,' the waiter asked, and for the first time a sliver of a smile passed between her and Declan, an indicator that he, too, vividly remembered the jokes they had shared, the memories of what had once bound them together.

She would come back to Melbourne from a long-haul flight utterly exhausted but never too tired to end up at Declan's. He would run her a bath, massage her aching feet and ankles and listen as she rambled on about her job—how tired she was, how difficult the passengers had been.

'Come on, Lila,' he would say with a laugh, 'you love every minute.'

'I know,' she would grudgingly admit, not wanting the massage to end. 'But it is tiring.'

'What? Asking whether they want chicken or beef?'

Indignantly she'd snatched her foot away. 'It is hard.'

'Then lie there and I'll fix dinner.' After kissing her deeply, Declan had disappeared off into the kitchen, only to return half an hour later dressed only in an apron and carrying two plates.

'Chicken or beef?' he had asked as she'd dozed peacefully on the sofa.

Wakening and seeing him there looking so ridiculously gorgeous she hadn't been able to stop laughing for a moment.

'I've got a far better idea,' Lila had said huskily, pulling at the apron. 'How about we join the mile-high club? Why don't you show me to your cabin?' As the meal was cleared the music struck up, Lila sat there for a moment, suddenly feeling exposed as her friends got up with their partners to dance. A wallflower certainly wasn't the image she wanted Declan to see.

'Finally.' Jez made his way over. 'How about a dance?'

He was tall, good-looking, funny even, but he was the wrong man, and it was the wrong man's arms that she was in. But it would have been rude to refuse and at least it saved her the embarrassment of being alone.

'I was hoping you'd be here tonight.'

When she didn't answer Jez continued, 'I was hoping we could dance.'

The music played on. Looking over his shoulder,

she saw Declan and Yvonne. As if sensing he was being watched, Declan's gaze flicked over in her direction, their eyes locking across the room. For a moment there was no Jez, no Yvonne, no one else in the room, just Declan and Lila and the sensual beat of the ballad that was playing.

'I meant what I said the other night—about dinner, I mean.'

Dragging her eyes away from Declan, Lila forced herself to look at Jez.

Why not say yes? Why not live for now, put the past where it belonged?

But, as nice as Jez was, he wasn't Declan.

Declan might belong to someone else, but her heart wasn't free. It would be wrong to lead Jez on.

'It's nice of you to ask, Jez, but...' Her voice trailed off as she tried to come up with a reason.

'Is that a no?'

Lila nodded. 'Sorry.'

'I'll survive.' He turned his head to where Lila's eyes lingered. 'Is that the reason? He doesn't waste any time, does he? He's only been here a couple of weeks.'

She hesitated before answering, yet she felt Jez deserved some sort of explanation.

'We go back a bit further than that,' she said finally.

As the music ended he let her go, kissing her

lightly on the cheek. 'Good luck,' he whispered into her ear. 'But watch yourself. I'd say you've got a fair bit of competition there.'

If Lila's ego had needed a boost that night, it got one. Again and again she was asked to dance, even a couple more offers of dinner were politely declined. But the one person she wanted to dance with, and she admitted reluctantly the real reason she was here, was studiously ignoring her.

'Well, more fool me for asking you to come,' Sue said as they collapsed at the table and took a grateful sip of their drinks. 'How are the rest of us supposed to get a look-in when you turn up looking stunning?'

Not stunning enough obviously.

'Fancy another drink?'

Lila nodded. 'Thanks, Sue.'

Alone at the table again, her eyes moved to Declan once more. He was talking to Mr Hinkley, chatting and laughing, every bit the dashing young doctor on the way up. And from what Declan had said during that bitter exchange in Lila's office, she could have been there with him. Had she been so wrong that day? Had she read him so wrong? Overreacted too violently, made the biggest mistake of her life?

Had she?

The answer was immaterial now. It was simply too late. He had Yvonne; he had brought her to the other side of the world to be beside him.

The threatening sting of tears suddenly pricked her eyes. She couldn't cry here, couldn't embarrass herself that way.

Making her way to the toilet, she changed course quickly as she saw Yvonne teetering in that direction rather ungracefully. Yvonne was the last person she wanted to make small talk with. Instead she slipped out into the foyer and stepped out onto the balcony.

The cool night air was welcome and she took a few calming breaths, looking out unseeingly at the dark night sky. A storm was breaking to the east— flashes of lightning flickering in the distance, the rumble of far-away thunder. The music was pounding away inside, and as the tempo changed and the achingly familiar beat of Declan's and her favourite song struck up Lila couldn't hold back the tears any longer.

'There you are.'

She didn't move, didn't turn around. He wasn't going to see her cry.

'I just wanted to get some air,' she said, trying to keep her voice even. 'It's a bit smoky in there.' Quickly she wiped her cheeks.

'Lila.' His hand was on her shoulder, his touch so, so familiar that she felt a nearly overwhelming urge to put her hand over his, to draw him nearer.

'We still haven't had that dance.'

She turned to face him, just a hand space separating them. The music seemed to be speaking to her, reminding her of how good it had been. Placing his whisky carefully on the stone wall of the balcony, he turned back to her, his fingers gently tilting her chin. And as her eyes met his, she knew she was lost.

Melting into his arms, they swayed slowly to the music. The warmth of his body, the silent strength in his embrace, the male scent of him—all played their part in peeling the years away.

'I've never stopped missing you,' he murmured. 'You've been on my mind every day.'

Closing her eyes, she leant even further into him. She could hear the thumping of his heart in his chest.

'I've missed you, too,' Lila admitted.

And *how* she had missed him. Missed the way he'd held her, the way he'd loved her. The undisguised admiration in his eyes when he'd looked at her, the way he'd made her laugh, made her feel. How he'd turned any situation around and seen the lighter side, but serious too when it had been merited.

Had she misjudged him so badly? Had she said goodbye to the best thing in her life over a stupid misunderstanding?

She knew when the music ended they should have left it there. That she should have thanked him and gone inside. And that had been her intention. But as she looked up to speak, as their eyes met and held, the words just wouldn't come. Her lips weren't moving to her command. Instead, they moved with instinct, back to the familiar, exciting place they had been so many times before. Yet now there was nothing safe in familiarity. His cool tongue gently exploring her mouth, the scratch of his cheek against hers, the intake of his breath as he pulled her nearer.

Her body blossomed beneath him. She felt as if champagne were running through her veins, tiny bubbles exploding as her breasts tingled, her stomach tightening in a reflex action to his touch. And he felt it, too. She could feel his inflamed desire pressing into her and she ground her hips against him.

With breathtaking stealth his hands travelled along her body, and she felt herself melt beneath his touch. Her hands were lost in his thick hair and she kissed him back with longing. Slowly, deliberately his fingers moved to her zip, achingly close to her swollen breast. She was filled with a brazen longing for him to inch down the zipper, to slip his long warm fingers inside and touch her aching breasts. But not here. Declan would never compromise her in that way.

His fingers lingered just a moment, almost teasing her with what could be if only she let it. He pulled away, staring at her for the longest time.

'I remember this dress,' he said huskily. 'Hell, Lila, I remember everything about you.'

The sound of the balcony door opening gave them

only the tiniest chance to break apart. With horror Lila realised it was Yvonne.

Utter shame swept over her. Never in a million years had this been her intention, but it was too late for regrets. The consequences of her actions had to be faced.

Yvonne hadn't just had a bit too much to drink, she was teetering unsteadily, her eyes angry and confused. 'What are you doing out here?'

'Talking to Lila.'

'Well, I'm sorry if I've disturbed you.' The contempt in Yvonne's voice was painfully obvious.

Unable to meet the other woman's eye, Lila looked down at the ground, painfully aware that Declan was wearing rather a lot of her lipstick at that moment.

'Mr Hinkley suggested that some of the *doctors* head off to the casino. I thought it might be fun.'

'Do you want me to call you a taxi?' he suggested, deliberately misreading what Yvonne had said.

Lila looked up sharply, amazed at his response. He seemed neither guilty nor perturbed that Yvonne had come so close to catching them, maybe even had. Who knew what she had seen as she'd approached the balcony? It didn't take an Einstein to work out what had gone on.

'Look, I'm sorry to break up your private party,'

she said nastily, 'but Mr Hinkley is your boss, not mine. Surely it would be better for your career…'

'My career's fine, Yvonne,' Declan said darkly. 'And the best thing you could do for yours is have a strong black coffee and go home to bed.'

'You bastard.'

'Yvonne…' Lila's voice was shaky. 'I can explain. Look, I'm really sorry…'

But Yvonne wasn't interested in hearing what Lila had to say. 'You're welcome to him,' she spat at Lila, and with a sob fled from the balcony back into the party.

Lila stood, stunned. 'You'd better go to her.'

'Let her go,' he said angrily. 'I'm sick of her dramas.'

'I'd say she had every reason to be upset. Just go after her, Declan. Don't make it any worse than it is.'

She was utterly bemused by his reaction, and even more so when he turned to face her again, pulling her back into his arms. 'Now, where were we?'

Aghast, she pushed him away. 'How dare you? How dare you?' She repeated. 'No wonder Yvonne's drunk. Any woman would need a general anaesthetic to put up with you. You have the audacity to follow me out here, to kiss me, to—'

'I don't recall much resistance. In fact, from where I was standing—'

Lila had never hit a man in her life, never hit anyone, in fact. It was against all her principles. But so was Declan Haversham, so was a man who could so openly play with her affections. So recklessly destroy Yvonne. As her hand aimed for his cheek she was so blinded with anger and rage that principles were the last thing on her mind.

But Declan was too quick for her. Grabbing her wrist, he held her outstretched hand in the air and she stood there, fury blazing in her blue eyes.

'Funny,' he said slowly, 'I really thought you'd grown up at last.' He released his grip and, shocked and reeling from her outburst, she stood there mute as Declan continued. 'I guess it will take a bit more than a nursing degree to change the self-centred, spoiled little madam you always were.'

She ran a tongue over her dry lips. 'Meaning?'

'Just that.' He spat the words at her. 'It was always about you, wasn't it? "I'm tired, Declan."' He mimicked her voice. 'Never mind that I'd been studying all week and maybe needed to let off a bit of a steam. But when I was tired it was a different story, wasn't it? Never mind I'd spent a week in lectures and four nights at the hospital. If little Lila wanted to party because her airline friends were in town, well, party time it was.

'And you haven't changed a bit. "Let's be friends, Declan" and twenty-four hours later you change your mind. "I've missed you, Declan. Kiss me, Declan" and the next minute you're slapping my face. I've had a bellyfull of you, Lila Bailey. I'm up to here with you.' His hand jabbed at his neck.

'Now, if you'll excuse me, my drunken housemate needs a lift to the casino and the obliging guy I am looks like I'm going to be playing taxi.'

'Your housemate?'

Declan paused, his shoulder rigid as he turned. 'That's right.'

'But I thought…' Lila said slowly. 'I mean, Yvonne said that you and she…' Her voice trailed off.

'Yvonne said what?' His voice was suddenly menacing. 'Come on, Lila, Yvonne said what exactly?'

'She said that you were on together, that you were living together.'

'She said that?'

Lila nodded.

'You didn't mishear. I mean, you didn't just take it the wrong way?'

The shock in his voice was so raw that unless Declan had done a double degree in drama and medicine, Lila knew this was a revelation.

She shook her head grimly as he stood there, staring at her. 'No, I didn't mishear, Declan. Yvonne was very clear in what she said.'

'But why would she say such a thing?'

'You tell me.' Although Lila had been proven wrong the animosity of the argument still hung in the air, the anger of a few moments ago hadn't quite abated. 'Perhaps you led her on, too.'

'Led her on? Is that what you think I did to you? When am I supposed to have led you on, Lila? Come on, you can't throw a pearl like that at me and not back it up.'

'Let her think you cared about her, loved her even.'

His whisky was sitting on the wall and he reached for it. Swirling the amber liquid around the heavy glass, he shook his head. 'Perhaps I did,' he said slowly. 'Maybe I should have seen this coming, but to compare Yvonne to you and me…' He exhaled deeply. 'Well, it doesn't compare.' He looked up, his eyes dark hollows in the shadows of the night. 'The difference is I did love you, Lila, did care about you.' He moved forward an inch. 'The saddest part of it all is that I still do…' He laughed, but it was so shallow Lila knew he didn't mean it.

'I really ought to give her a lift, though, or heaven knows where she'll end up.'

'Oughtn't you to take her home?'

'She a big girl, she can take care of herself. And anyway, Mr Hinkley's pretty gone himself so I doubt he'll even notice how out of it she is. I'd better go now…' But he didn't move. Lila could hear him jangling his car keys in his jacket pocket as if weighing up whether or not to continue. 'Come on,' he said eventually. 'I think we need to talk.'

Yvonne really was the worse for wear. Thankfully she had extracted herself from the party and was sitting somewhat forlornly on one of the planters at the front of the hotel.

'You stay with her,' Declan instructed. 'I'll go and bring the car around.'

'Would you rather we get a taxi?' Lila suggested. 'In case you've had too much to drink.'

She had seen him angry, seen him annoyed and irritated, but she had never seen such contempt emanating from the steely grey eyes as he faced her. 'Lila,' he said, his voice deathly quiet, his cheeks quilted with tension, 'I did grow up. I'm not the twenty-something medical student you seem to recall. I'm an emergency registrar now. Do you really think I'd be so stupid as to get behind the wheel loaded?'

'Of course not. I was just making sure.'

'Well, there's no need. Unlike some people I could mention, some of us grew up a while ago.'

As he stormed off to the car park she stood there trembling and confused. Somehow she had got it all wrong.

'I'm sorry.' Yvonne's voice broke into her confused thoughts. 'I've ruined your night.'

Lila sat down on the planter beside Yvonne. 'Don't worry about it. I think it was ruined long ago.'

'Declan's going to be furious with me…'

'If it's any consolation, he's furious with me as well. Yvonne, I'm sorry if it's none of my business, but I really need to know what's going on. Is there anything between you and Declan? If there is I can only apologise for what happened…'

Yvonne put up a rather unsteady hand. 'Honestly, there's nothing to apologise for.'

'But you did say that you and Declan were an item. If you've got some sort of—I don't know—open relationship…'

'We don't have a relationship. Not for the want of trying on my part, though.'

'I'm sorry.'

'No, you're not,' Yvonne said, and some of her earlier venom returned. 'But I haven't finished yet. I didn't come from the other side of the world to be beaten by an ex from eight years ago.'

'It isn't a competition,' Lila reasoned.

'Isn't it?'

'Of course not. And anyway, Declan and I were over years ago.'

'Good.' Yvonne stood up as headlights lit up her face. 'And I intend to keep it that way.'

The hooting of the car prevented Lila from responding, not that there was much that she could have said. Instead, she sat awkwardly in the back of the car after Yvonne jumped like a scalded cat into the front seat. Lila couldn't have cared less where she sat—the back suited her fine. At least the journey gave her a little time to collect her thoughts. Her heart was hammering, her mind whirring. Nothing tonight made any sense, but, then, why should it? Since Declan had appeared on the scene she had been spun into utter confusion.

Even when he dropped Yvonne off at the casino, Lila remained in the back, sitting in silence as Declan glided the car through the deserted Melbourne streets.

She was somewhat taken aback when he let her inside his house. Lila cast a look around. It was a classic Melbourne townhouse—beautifully refurbished, polished floorboards lining the hallway and stairs, lead light windows filtering the glow from the lamppost outside.

'Are you and Yvonne renting together?' They were the first words she had spoken to him since the bitter exchange outside the hotel.

'I own it,' he said curtly. 'Why do you look so surprised? Were you expecting a students' dive? Like I told you, I've come on a bit since then.' He climbed down off his high horse. Bragging really wasn't Declan's style and Lila knew his tirade would be short-lived. 'Actually, I own it, along with the bank.'

He managed a sheepish grin. 'But at least I keep this place tidy.' Running a hand through his hair for the first time since their paths had crossed again Declan actually appeared uncomfortable.

'I don't know about you but I could really use a drink right now. Can I get you one?'

Lila nodded, following him though to the kitchen.

Years might have passed and, yes, they might have changed, but as he opened the fridge and went to pull out a bottle of white wine he immediately closed it again.

'Sorry.' Taking a bottle of Lila's preferred red from the wine rack, he started to open it as Lila rather shakingly took two glasses from the overhead cupboards.

It felt strange, surreal, both of them in a kitchen opening a bottle. It reeked of yesterday, felt so…so familiar that it hurt, it actually hurt.

He carried the glasses through to the lounge, waiting till Lila was seated on the sofa before passing her glass to her then joining her on the couch.

'Yvonne and I aren't together. We never have been,' he said when the silence had gone on for far too long.

'Then why did she say that you were?'

'You tell me.' When Lila didn't respond he cast around for answers. 'Maybe she likes me…'

'Likes you?' Lila actually laughed. 'Oh, believe

me, Declan, she likes you all right. The woman's followed you to other side of the world, for heaven's sake!'

'Come on Lila, she's not that bad. I think she just had a bit too much to drink tonight. Perhaps Yvonne thought if she said that we were on together, it might...' He didn't finish the sentence. Instead, he chose the safety of his wineglass.

'Might what?' Lila prompted.

'Might stop us from getting back together. You see, Lila, I told her about us ages ago when we were still in Scotland. And whatever you think, she really didn't like me then, at least not in that way. We were just friends. I wanted to move home and she'd applied for a job in Melbourne—there was nothing more to it than that. Of course I said that she could stay with me for a while, at least until she found her feet. If Yvonne has been acting differently then it's only in the last few weeks or so. Maybe she's homesick or a bit lonely. And I guess if she has got a crush on me it must have been a pretty tough couple of weeks for her, what with me banging on about you all the time.'

'You've been talking about me?'

'Of course I've been talking about you, Lila, you're all I've been going on about for the last few weeks, all I've been talking about since I finally made up my mind to come back home. Hell, I was hoping to bump into you at the shops one day or on the beach perhaps—but working alongside you, I couldn't have planned that if I'd tried. I've been bending Yvonne's ear, asking her if she thought there was a chance…'

He stopped talking, unsaid words hanging in the air, teasing her with the impossibility of what he might have been about to say.

His finger was running around the rim of his glass and he cleared his throat before he continued. 'A chance for us. Whether we might be able to make things work this time around.'

Did they have a chance? From the few exchanges they'd shared it was obvious there was a lot of hurt there, a lot of damage already inflicted. And the world had changed so much since then. They were two different people now. Older if not wiser. With different goals and dreams. She sat quite still, watching his finger travelling aimlessly around the glass.

She should have left it there, waited for the morning to think things through, to open up and share with him how difficult her life was now, how a relationship with him, with anyone, in fact, was impossible.

But she didn't.

This night was for them. Tomorrow could wait a while. Just to feel his arms around her again, feel the weight of his kiss…

She simply couldn't let the moment pass. Tomorrow was an age away…

Leaning forward slightly, Lila took the glass from his hand, stretching over to place it on the coffeetable. She felt his eyes move, felt the weight of his gaze on her creamy cleavage, heard him swallow. He had always loved her breasts. His eyes moved quickly to hers but she knew he was aroused, knew that he wanted her, too.

She saw a flicker of uncertainty in his features, and she knew she should also feel it. But right now she needed to forget. Forget the problems, forget the pain, and let Declan make it all right, like he always had before.

'Lila?' His voice was husky, questioning, and she silenced him with a kiss, but he gently pulled back. 'Are you sure?'

That they wouldn't hurt in the morning?

No.

That she was doing the right thing?

Probably not.

That she wanted him?

Yes.

Oh, yes.

Taking his hand, she guided it to her dress, closing her eyes as he slowly pulled down the zipper.

'I'm sure, Declan,' she said, her voice thick with need. 'I'm sure.'

*   *   *

Familiarity bred contempt.

It didn't.

At least not when the hands that were holding you, touching you, were so attuned that they moved instinctively where they were needed.

When the mouth that moved slowly, teasingly across your stomach and up to your engorged and aching breasts knew when you couldn't take restraint any more.

As the rough scratch of his thighs pushed between her legs, her body arched beneath him, desperate for a deeper closeness, desperate to seal their union.

He knew how much she needed him, wanted him, yet he made her wait. Made her wait until her long nails were digging into his muscular buttocks, until she was urging him to enter her sweet welcoming warmth.

And when finally he did, when he gave way to the primaeval instincts that engulfed him, Lila cried out in surrender, abandoning herself to the waves that swept over her. There was no need to wait now, no need for holding back, and they couldn't have if they'd tried. They had waited for this moment long enough.

The oblivion she had craved came then. Nothing else mattered for that moment, just the exquisite pleasure that was hers and Declan's alone.

And after as he led her to his bed, laying her down

with infinite tenderness, for the longest time he held her. Stroking her, massaging her, touching her, loving her with such reverence, taking their time to get to know each other's bodies all over again.

CHAPTER FIVE

DECLAN, I have to go home now. Mum will need to
be turned.

Declan, I normally turn Mum at six. I ought to be
getting back.

Lila lay in the darkness, staring at the clock, the
weight of Declan's arm solid and warm, trying to
fathom how to tell Declan she needed to head for
home. But no matter how she said it, it sounded
wrong.

How could he even begin to understand?

What possible chance was there of them having a
relationship? It was hard enough now, but in six short
weeks Ted would retire, and that rendered it practically impossible.

Declan and Elizabeth had never got on in the past.
Elizabeth had hated him with a passion, and Declan,
well, he had tolerated her. Tolerated her idiosyncra-
sies, her constant snipes at him, with as much humour as he could muster.

Elizabeth was way past that now—in fact, she
never spoke—but why should Declan turn his life
around for a woman who had despised him? And if
they were to have a relationship, that was what it

would entail—a total turn-around. No spontaneous checking into luxury hotels after romantic dinners. No spur-of-the-moment trips. Every moment of Elizabeth's day had to be accounted for. How could Lila possibly land it on him?

She should have told him all of this yesterday, should have laid things on the line before they had gone this far.

But... Lila squeezed her eyes closed against the tears that were forming. She could never regret what had taken place. The solace she had found in his arms, the utter peace she had felt after they'd made love, would carry her through the uncertain months and years ahead.

Had she used him?

Yes.

Her only defence was that she loved him.

As she inched away his arm that was protectively draped around her, she held her breath as Declan gave a mumble of protest in his sleep. Only when she was sure he had settled again did Lila ease herself out of the bed, creeping quietly into the lounge where her discarded clothes lay. Shivering as she pulled on her underwear and slipped on her dress and shoes, Lila decided to use her mobile phone rather than risk waking Declan by using the hall phone. Unsure of the house number, Lila gave the street to the taxi company and said she'd wait outside.

'What are you doing?'

The light flooded the room, making her blink as she stood there as guilty as if he had caught her going through his wallet.

Declan stared at her for a moment before crossing the room and taking the mobile from her. 'Cancel the taxi order, thank you.' His voice was curt. Clicking off the phone, he handed it back to Lila, his eyes questioning.

'I have to get home.'

'Then why didn't you wake me? I'd have taken you.'

'You were sleeping.' She fumbled for excuses.

'That's what people do at four in the morning Lila. What's so important that you have to get back?'

Lila shrugged. 'I just do, that's all.'

'Come on Lila, you're thirty years old now. You never had to rush home eight years ago, so what's changed? Unless, of course, you were hoping to avoid me.'

'I…' She stood there, mouthing silently. 'Thirty-one actually.'

'What?'

Lila gave a nervous laugh. 'You said I was thirty years old, I was just saying I'm actually thirty-one.'

'Do you want me to sing ''Happy Birthday''? Perhaps we should have a make-up class for all the bloody birthdays and Christmases you made us miss out on?'

And though she was fully clothed, while Declan stood there naked as the day he was born, it was Lila that felt uncomfortable. She looked at his face, saw the hurt, the utter confusion, and she knew it was time for the truth.

'I have to get back to my mum, Declan. She's not too well.'

'So why didn't you tell me?' he rasped. 'Did you think I wouldn't understand? Did you think stealing out of bed and creeping off in the middle of the night was a better way of going about things?'

'No.'

'Then why, Lila?' He ran a hand through his hair and his eyes burned with unanswered questions. He had never looked more gorgeous in her eyes, or more unattainable.

'What aren't you telling me?'

'Work it out, Declan,' she choked. 'You're the doctor, work it out for yourself.' Her voice was rising now. 'It's been eight years since Mum was diagnosed. She's not the woman she was. I'm going home to wet sheets and pressure-area care, and after that I'll try and cajole her into taking a few mouthfuls of porridge. That gets me to eight a.m. You say you understand, but how can you? I'm not free to have a relationship, not free to be with you.'

'We can work something out, Lila,' he reasoned. 'Together.'

She shook her head. 'What, you'll find a terribly nice home for her? For my benefit, of course.'

'I didn't say that. There must be some solution.'

Her hands shot up to her ears, a childish gesture she hadn't used in decades.

'Stop it!' she shouted. 'Stop it. There isn't a solution, Declan.'

He grabbed her hands, pulling them away from her ears and forcing her wrists to her sides. 'We can work something out.' His words were loud, sharp, but devoid of any anger. 'We can, Lila,' he pleaded. 'If we want to be together then we'll work something out and get through this.'

She didn't dare hope, didn't dare believe there could be an answer. She hadn't even told him the worst of it, that in six weeks they might be looking for a new home.

She couldn't let them get back together only to break up later, couldn't bear to go through the pain she had endured all over again. The agony of watching their relationship die a slow and painful death was more than Lila could bear. Better the quick relief of a mortal wound. 'Maybe I don't want that.' She watched him flinch. 'Maybe I don't want to be with you.'

'But before…' He gestured to the sofa. 'Didn't that mean anything to you?'

'We had sex, Declan, good sex, and that was all that I wanted from you. Let's just leave it at that, shall we?' She hated hurting him, hated what she was saying, but it was kinder this way. Kinder than the truth. Taking on Lila would change his life. It simply wouldn't be fair. 'I didn't come looking for a ring. Now, can I have my mobile back so I can ring for a taxi?'

He didn't let her get a taxi. Instead, he pulled on some old jeans, a T-shirt and runners. He might be too responsible to drink but there was nothing mature about the way he accelerated out of the driveway.

He accepted her directions without comment. Pulling up outside her aunt's house, he stared out of the windscreen as Lila pulled off her seat belt.

'I'm sorry,' she said, her hand on the door handle. 'But it really is better this way.'

He turned to face her, his lip curling with distaste as he looked at her.

'I mean it this time, Lila.' His voice was like ice. 'I'm through trying to work you out. Do you know what I hate about all this the most?'

When she didn't answer he continued bitterly. 'I hate the fact that I'm as much to blame for all this as you are. I've let you walk over me again and again but this time I'm finished. I'm totally over you, Lila.'

As she stepped out of the car he sent his parting shot.

'Have a nice life, Lila.'

Through her tears, Lila managed a smile as she let herself in. The lounge looked like a bomb had hit it, the video still whirring away, half-drunk glasses of wine on the table, an empty box of chocolates. At least Ted and Shirley had had a good night.

Wincing at the creak, she opened her mother's bedroom door. Creeping over to the bed, she perched on the edge.

'Oh, Mum.' The real tears came then, not loud, just muffled, agonised sobs as she held Elizabeth's hand. But Elizabeth's hand didn't tighten on hers. She didn't take her daughter in her arms and soothe her child. Promise that things would be better soon, that there was a reason for this pain. There was no comfort because there was none to be had. Her mother was gone, as surely as if she had died.

As she slipped into her own bed, Lila closed her eyes and let the one comfort she had left in life hold her close. The memory of Declan's arms around her. She had been wrong tonight. Wrong to use him, knowing it could go nowhere, yet as she remembered the passion and tenderness of their love-making she couldn't regret it...

*   *   *

There were a lot of eyes avoiding each other on Monday night.

Declan didn't even bother to be polite and pointedly called her 'Sister', even then only speaking when he absolutely had to.

Yvonne was blushing at every turn, not sure who knew and what had been said.

Sue was equally jumpy, darting out off the nurses' station every time Lila even came near.

During a quiet moment, as Lila tackled the never-ending problem that was the roster, she called Sue back when her colleague did a sudden about-turn, realising Lila was at the desk.

'For heaven's sake, Sue,' Lila finally confronted her. 'What on earth's going on? Look, I'm sorry I disappeared. I know I asked you to get me a drink…'

'It's not that.' Sue blushed.

'Then what?'

'You won't be cross?'

'Just tell me,' Lila demanded. 'It's like working in a minefield here.'

'Well, the bar closed soon after I got your drink and, well, when you didn't come back…'

'Sue!'

'All right. Jez wanted a drink. I gave him yours and, well, one thing sort of led to another. We went out last night. Look, I don't want to tread on your toes—'

Lila laughed. 'You're not.'

'Truly.'

'No, in fact, I'm delighted for you both.'

'So what happened to you, then? Where did you disappear to?'

'I just had enough all of a sudden.'

'Hmm.' Sue gave her a sceptical look. 'If you say so. Anyway, I got one thing right. Declan and Yvonne are hardly talking. He looks like he's about to explode he's so angry. I've never seen him like this. Declan's normally so friendly. She must have really upset him.'

Lila certainly wasn't about to enlighten Sue.

'Lila, can I have a hand?'

'Sure, Lucy.' Glad to end the conversation, Lila jumped down off her stool, closing the roster book shut with a snap.

'It's Jessica Stevens, the overdose patient.'

'What's the problem?' Jessica had taken a large number of analgesics some hours ago and had arrived in the department a short time before. Given the time that had passed since her overdose, washing her stomach out would have proved pointless so it had been decided to give her some Carbomix—a black charcoal drink that lined the stomach and bowel and prevented further absorption of the medicines she had taken.

'She's extremely agitated and refusing to drink the

mixture.' That often happened. Overdose patients were often distressed and in some cases disorientated.

'Has the doctor explained the consequences of refusing treatment?' Lila asked as she flicked through the casualty card.

'Well Declan has, but her husband has just arrived with some more empty bottles. It would seem she's Amitriptyline as well as the other pills and alcohol. I'm just not happy with her, Lila.'

Lila grimaced. Amitriptyline was a particularly nasty drug that, when taken in excess, could cause cardiac arrhythmias. And Lucy's ominous statement about not being happy with the patient was enough to ring a warning bell in Lila's head.

'OK, let's get her over to Resus and on a monitor. I'll talk to her. Can you go and accept the patient the paramedics are wheeling in? Just let me know if there are any concerns.'

'Sure.' Lila liked working with Lucy. Although she had just completed her grad year, Lucy had already developed a sixth sense for when something wasn't quite right. It was an essential tool all good Emergency nurses possessed and one that wasn't easily defined. A hunch perhaps that, despite what the observation chart said, despite how the patient looked, there was something more sinister going on.

Lucy, also more than happy to defer to her superiors when necessary, another essential tool when building a strong and co-operative nursing team.

Jessica was extremely upset, crying and thrashing about.

'Mrs Stevens.' Lila patted her shoulder. 'Jessica, my name is Lila Bailey. I'm the nurse in charge to-night. I've been told you don't want to take the Carbomix.'

'It's disgusting.'

Jessica's teeth were black from her previous attempts at drinking the mixture.

'I know, but it really is practically tasteless, and it's imperative that you have it.' Lila was working quickly as she spoke, clipping the cardiac monitor to the red dots she had placed on the woman's chest.

'She has to have it,' the medical registrar stated unhelpfully, only inflaming Jessica's anger even further.

'I don't have to do anything! You can't make me!'

Jessica was upset, distressed, but Lila felt she wasn't beyond reason. 'No, Jessica, we can't make you. You have every right to refuse treatment. However, refusing treatment could end your life.' She stared directly at the distraught woman. 'You could die, Jessica.'

'I took a few too many painkillers...'

'Enough to do serious damage.' Lila's voice was more insistent now. She was also acutely aware that

Declan had joined them. As the senior doctor on that night he had every right to be there, every right to ensure things were going all right, but his appearance did nothing to help Lila. She focussed her attention on the patient.

'I'm not drinking that sludge.'

'OK, fair enough, but what if we passed a soft tube into your stomach and gave you the drink through that? You wouldn't have to taste it then.' She glanced up at the medical registrar, who nodded.

'Is that going to hurt?'

Lila took her patient's hand. It was imperative she keep Jessica's confidence. Lying wasn't going to achieve that.

'It won't hurt, Jessica, but it will be uncomfortable. A soft rubber tube will be passed through your nose into your stomach—that's the uncomfortable bit. Once it's in place it won't hurt at all.'

'And you'll do it?' Jessica looked over to the med reg. 'He's not coming near me.'

'Jessica, I'll do it, but it really is imperative that it's done soon.'

Passing a nasogastric tube was a basic procedure, but with a conscious patient it required some degree of co-operation and patience. Neither of which Jessica possessed tonight.

'Page me when her bloods come back' was the total of the med reg's contribution to the procedure.

Lila had passed NG tubes numerous times, and not just at work. Sometimes, when Elizabeth was particularly difficult to feed and she was starting to become dehydrated, rather than having her admitted to hospital for an intravenous infusion, Lila would pass a tube and give her mother some extra fluids.

But Elizabeth Bailey in her twilight world was a different patient entirely to Jessica, who thrashed around, gagging and pulling the tube, resisting all efforts.

'Here.' Declan saw she was struggling. 'Jessica, I'm going to hold your hands so you're not tempted to pull at the tube when Nurse Bailey passes it.'

Not a look passed between them and, as uncomfortable as his presence made her, Lila was grateful for his help.

'Is it in?' he asked as Lila listened with her stethoscope to Jessica's stomach. Pushing air into the tube with a syringe allowed you to hear the air gurgling in the stomach, ensuring the tube was safely in place. Only Lila couldn't hear it. 'I don't think so. It didn't go in easily. I think I should reinsert it.'

Jessica had calmed down now, but this did nothing to reassure Lila.

'She's becoming drowsy.'

'Chest X-ray.' The radiographer announced from the corridor as he arrived with his portable machine.

'Over here, thanks,' Declan called. 'Let them do

the film and then take out the tube and have another go. Is there anything else she might have taken?' he asked as they put on the lead gowns the radiographer passed them. Jessica was too unwell to be left alone.

'Not sure.' Lila frowned. 'Her husband's had a lot to drink. He's taken a taxi home to check for any other tablets that might be missing. Hopefully he'll ring soon.'

'Well, let's get the Carbomix into her—I'm not too happy. Where's the med reg?'

'Guess.'

'On the wards?'

Lila nodded.

'OK, pass the tube again and I'll give him a friendly call.' The wry note in his voice didn't go unnoticed.

The tube was easy to pass this time. Jessica was complacent now. Listening with her stethoscope, though sure it was now in place Lila still aspirated some fluid, testing it on litmus paper. The colour change on the litmus paper due to the acidic contents of the stomach was a further safeguard.

'You in?' Declan asked, coming over.

'Listen for me?'

He did as asked, and Lila pushed some more air down the tube as Declan placed his stethoscope over Jessica's stomach. 'Gurgling away,' he stated, pulling his stethoscope out of his ears. 'Put the Carbomix down and I'll ring the lab, see if there's any more of her bloods back.'

It took only a moment to pass the Carbomix down the tube. Jessica's consciousness level was definitely decreasing and Lila popped her head out into the corridor as Declan returned from his telephone call.

'Lucy, come into Resus, I've a feeling we might be needing you soon. What did the lab say?' she asked as he made his way back.

But Declan didn't answer. Moving forward, he suddenly spoke loudly to the patient, rubbing his hand on her sternum as he did so to initiate some kind of response.

'Mrs Stevens.'

Lila looked at the monitor as she felt for the patient's pulse. It was strong and rapid but she wasn't breathing. In one fluid movement Lila pulled down the headrest of the trolley and started to bag the patient.

'Put out a call,' she instructed Lucy.

Declan had reached for a large syringe, quickly pulling back the Carbomix Lila had so recently put down in a desperate bid to empty Jessica's stomach as Lila inflated her patient's lungs with air.

'Her pupils are pinpoint,' Declan stated as he flashed a light into Jessica's eyes.

He looked up at Lila for a second.

'Lucy, pull up some Narcan.'

Declan hadn't even needed to say it, she knew what he was thinking. He nodded his agreement as Lucy passed the drug that would reverse any narcotics Jessica might have taken. Combined with alcohol, some drugs can lead to sudden respiratory arrest, and even though Jessica hadn't admitted to taking such a drug she was displaying obvious symptoms. Administering Narcan would do no harm if they were wrong, but if Jessica had indeed taken a narcotic overdose the drug might just save her life.

Narcan, when appropriate, works quickly, so quickly in fact that by the time the cardiac arrest team had arrived Jessica was back to her restless self.

'Respiratory arrest, guys. We just reversed it with Narcan—she must have also taken some opiates.'

Jessica was vomiting now. Despite her stomach having been speedily emptied, some of the Carbomix obviously remained.

'It's all right, Jessica,' Lila soothed. Holding Jessica's hair back, she felt her suddenly slump under her touch.

'She's gone again.'

Lucy handed over another syringe of Narcan as the anaesthetist suctioned her airway.

There was tension in the room. All were concerned, but this was a regular occurrence in Emergency and all the staff, apart from Lucy, were senior and used to dealing with such crises.

'She'll need a Narcan infusion,' Declan stated. 'While this drug's in her system she's just going to keep going off.'

'Her chest is a bit rattly,' the anaesthetist stated. 'She may well have aspirated. Look, I've got a bed on ICU and she'd probably be better off there. We'll get another chest X-ray first and I'll let the staff know.'

Of course, it was never that easy. ICU might have a bed but they needed another nurse to be pulled from the wards to cover it. And ICU-trained nurses were rarer than hen's teeth. Jessica was going to be there for a while.

Lila was glad to be busy, glad that the cubicles were full and there were plenty of patients on the board waiting to be seen. Glad she didn't have to face any uncomfortable silences with Declan.

She watched him, though, surreptitiously listening as he shot a few sharp words at the med reg or chatted amicably to a rather inebriated teenager he was stitching.

He was so in control, friendly but undoubtedly in charge, knowledgeable but never superior. If she hadn't loved him, Lila thought ruefully, Declan Haversham would be a sheer pleasure to work with.

They waded through the patients, waded through the long night. Emergency wasn't the kind of place you could avoid each other even if you wanted to.

Jessica settled down, so much so, in fact, that she no longer required the precious ICU bed, which heralded an even longer wait as a high-dependency bed was located. Checking her observations, Lila gave the patient a reassuring smile.

'Your observations are all stable, Jessica. As the doctor explained, we're waiting for a bed on the high-dependency unit, so I'm afraid it might take a while. I'm sorry. I know that you've been down here for ages.'

'That's all right.' Jessica lay back against the pillow. 'I'm just sorry I've put everyone to all this bother. I don't even feel sick, just a bit wobbly. I'd really rather just be at home.'

'Don't even think about it.' Lila gave the woman a smile. 'You really do need to be here. I know that now you might not feel too bad, but the tablets you've taken really can cause serious damage.'

'The doctor said that I stopped breathing before— is that true?'

Lila nodded. 'But luckily you were here when that happened. That's why it's imperative that you stay. And not just for the medication. Jessica, you took a lot of tablets. It's clear you've got some problems that need to be dealt with.'

'It's a bit late for all that.'

Lila didn't answer. She waited to see whether or

not Jessica chose to continue, not wanting to push at this fragile stage.

'We've been having a lot of problems, Mark and I.'

'Mark's your husband?'

Jessica nodded. 'Since the twins came along I just don't seem to be able to cope any more. He's always saying he doesn't mind the mess, doesn't mind that there's never any dinner on the table when he gets home from work. All he wants is for me to be happier.'

'He sounds nice.'

'He is nice. That's the whole problem.' Jessica started to cry. 'Too nice for me. He deserves better. He's bought us tickets to go to the theatre next weekend and then stay at some posh hotel. He thinks that if I have a break from the children…' She started to cry and Lila ran a washcloth under the tap in the cubicle, wiping the tears and streaks of Carbomix from Jessica's face. As Declan stepped into Resus Lila put a finger up to her lips, indicating for him to stay quiet. What Jessica had to say was important if she was going to get the appropriate treatment.

'He's lined up his mum to come from Adelaide for the weekend to babysit. He just doesn't understand that he's making things worse.'

'In what way?'

'How can I let his mum see the state the house is

in? How can I go to the theatre when I don't even fit into any of my dresses any more? Why doesn't he see how hard it is for me at the moment?'

The words were on Jessica's lips, but for a second she couldn't say them. Declan was staring at her, waiting her response.

But this wasn't about her and Declan, this was about helping Jessica. Even as she spoke Lila heard the tremor in her voice, heard the irony in her own words.

'Have you tried talking to him? Telling him how you're feeling?'

'He wouldn't understand,'

'He might,' Declan said gently. 'If you just let him in.'

Only the steady bleeping of the monitor broke the silence. Lila pulled a couple of tissues from a box and handed them to Jessica.

Suddenly she felt like crying herself.

'Anyway—' Declan's tone lightened '—we've finally found a bed for you—they're ready for her,' he added to Lila.

'Fine.' Lila forced a bright smile. 'Jessica, Lucy will take you up now. I have to stay down here.' Taking the other woman's hand, Lila gave her hand a squeeze. 'Take the help they offer you, Jessica. You might not think it now, but you've been very lucky tonight.'

She watched with a lump in her throat as Jessica was wheeled out of the department.

'How about you have a break?' Sue suggested. 'The department's practically empty. Declan's just stitching up the last couple.'

Gratefully Lila nodded. 'Sounds good to me.'

The television was always on in the staffroom, and Lila listlessly flicked the channels. Sue had just returned from her break and the blanket and pillow she had used were still lying temptingly warm on the sofa. Stretching out, Lila half watched the morning news in America, her eyelids suddenly heavy. Strange how that it was yesterday morning there. Wouldn't it be nice to start over like that? Rewind to Saturday morning and avoid the mess she'd made of her life on Saturday night.

But if she did that then she'd never have the precious memories that she had now.

Night staff often had a doze. The intercom soon buzzed if they were needed. Lila lay there, having changed into theatre blues after the mess from the Carbomix, pulling out her comb before she gave in and closed her eyes.

Lila never heard Declan come in and sit down. Stretching out on a chair with a yawn, he placed his tired, aching feet on the coffee-table. She never knew that as she lay there dozing, with her long limbs sprawled the length of the sofa, her blonde waves rippling over the pillow, Declan was silently watching her. Lila never even knew that as she lay there, dreaming of the other night, Declan's mind had wandered there, too.

Watching her sleep was a cruel reminder to him of how beautiful she had looked, and how much better life had seemed when her head had been resting on his pillow.

CHAPTER SIX

'NURSE BAILEY, could I have a word in my office?' Hester looked particularly crisp this morning.

'Sure, I'll just finish checking the drugs.'

Lila had been half expecting the summons. The applications had been in for two weeks now and she knew they were drawing up the short-list for interviews. Lila made her way to Hester's office and knocked briefly before entering.

'Have a seat, please.' She waited until Lila was seated before continuing. 'I've just had a call from the high-dependency unit.'

Lila frowned. This wasn't what she had been expecting.

'Did you insert an NG tube on a patient last night, name Jessica Stevens?'

'Yes.' Lila looked at her superior non-plussed.

'And did you ensure the tube was correctly positioned before giving the patient the Carbomix?'

'Of course.'

'Well, that's not what the X-ray shows.' Hester leant forward, her face menacing. 'The X-ray shows the tube entering the patient's lung. The same patient is now suffering from aspiration pneumonia.'

'But that's not due to me.' Lila shook her head in disbelief at the accusing tones in Hester's voice. 'The *first* tube I put down wasn't in correctly. It was *after* the X-ray that I reinserted the tube and gave the patient her medication. She was vomiting on admission and again during her respiratory arrest—that would have been when she aspirated.'

Hester threw the patient's casualty card across the table at Lila. 'Well, I've been looking at these notes for the last ten minutes and I can't find what you've just told me documented anywhere.'

Lila didn't need to see the notes to know that what Hester was saying was true. 'But we never document that sort of thing,' Lila argued. Surely Hester didn't think she was so irresponsible she would fail to check the tube was in place before administering anything down it?

'Correction,' Hester said menacingly. '*You*, Nurse Bailey, never document that sort of thing. And as a consequence I now have to go across to HDU and defend you on the basis of these flimsy notes.'

'There's nothing to defend. I did nothing wrong.'

Hester buzzed the intercom on her desk. 'Could Doctor Haversham please come to my office?'

She heard the protests from Moira, the charge nurse, but Hester was adamant. 'I don't care what he's doing. *Now*, Moira, please!'

Lila leant back in her chair with a sigh. This was

ridiculous, but it didn't stop her being nervous. She knew in her heart that she had done nothing wrong, and it was so typical of Hester, who always came down hard on her staff, more willing to believe any complaint was true than try listening to the defendant.

And now Declan was being dragged into it. Dragged into a petty argument between her and her boss.

It was utterly the last thing she needed now.

Declan arrived. To anyone else he would have appeared totally nonchalant and relaxed, but Lila knew him too well. The tiny furrow above his eyebrows showed Lila he was none too pleased to have been summoned.

'What's the problem, Hester? I'm actually in the middle of seeing a patient.'

'I shan't keep you long. I've just had the charge nurse on HDU ring down. She's preparing the notes and X-rays for the morning's round and she's noticed that Jessica Stevens had an NG tube incorrectly positioned. This same patient is now suffering form aspiration pneumonia.'

'I'm not surprised,' Declan said, his voice even and calm. 'She took a lot of tablets, suffered a respiratory arrest and, despite gastric emptying, vomited copiously. It's no wonder she inhaled some.'

'But as I pointed out, the X-rays showed—'

Declan stood up, looking first at Lila and then Hester.

'Have you discussed this with Lila?'

Hester nodded.

'What did she say?'

'I'd rather hear your version, Doctor. Nurse Bailey, perhaps you could wait in the staffroom for a moment while I speak to Dr Haversham.'

'There's no need for that. I've just been to HDU myself to check on Mrs Stevens. Good news travels fast in this place.' He gave a tight smile. 'Perhaps if you'd deigned to have a look at the more recent films yourself, Hester, you'd have realised the pneumonia is in the opposite lung to the misplaced tube. No mistakes were made last night.'

'None of this was documented.'

Declan turned for the door. 'Sorry about that,' he said glibly. 'We were a bit busy, saving her life. Now, if you'll excuse me, I'm going back to my patient.'

He shut the door firmly behind him, leaving Hester sitting at her desk, her cheeks and neck a rather un-flattering shade of red.

'It's not that I doubted you, Nurse Bailey. The point I was making was the fact that your actions last night weren't documented and that in turn leaves your actions open to misinterpretation.'

For an age Lila didn't answer. Surprisingly and

completely unexpectedly Lila felt tears prick at her eyes.

Declan had defended her, she'd known he would. Not because of what they had once been to each other but because she had done nothing wrong. Yet still it touched her. But Hester's accusatory tones had hurt, really hurt. Suddenly she felt tired, tired of the responsibility that came with each shift. Tired of the comradeship between colleagues, which Lila bolstered so passionately, that could so easily be eroded by a tyrannical boss.

'You're right, Hester,' Lila said finally. 'I should have documented what I did. Funny thing was, I was too busy talking to the patient. Too busy doing her obs and resuscitating her when she collapsed. Too busy finding out what had driven her to take the tablets in the first place.'

'We know how busy it is here, but notes are for the staff's protection.'

'And when are we supposed to write them, Hester? How in-depth do the notes need to be? I spent three years doing a degree, one year doing a critical-care course. I used all the safeguards in place when I inserted that tube, and the safeguards worked. I realised the tube wasn't in place and I reinserted it. That should be the end of the story. The sad part is that too many people are too quick to jump on a possible mistake. Too quick to assume the worse.'

Hester's flush meant Lila's words had hit their target, but Hester hadn't finished her lecture yet.

'I've also received the figures from the kitchen. Can you tell me why when you're in charge of the department there's a marked increase in the amount of breakfasts that are ordered?'

'Excuse me?'

'I'm not talking one or two here or there—see for yourself.' For the second time she thrust a sheaf of papers in Lila's direction. Again Lila didn't need to look, but the accusation that came from Hester's lips took the wind out of even Lila's sails. 'Are you ordering breakfast for the staff?'

The suggestion was so ludicrous that Lila gave an incredulous laugh.

'You think we'd risk our jobs for two slices of cold toast and a cup of weak tea?'

'Well, I can't think of any other reason. We'll leave it there, but I'll be watching the breakfast orders more closely from now on, the documentation, too. Things seem a little slack when you're in charge, Nurse Bailey.'

Lila picked up her bag wearily and made her way out of the office.

'How did it go?' Declan avoided meeting her eyes.

'Fine, I guess. She believed *you*, of course.' Lila let out a weary sigh. 'Declan, do you think I was wrong not to document what happened with the NG tube?'

Declan shrugged. 'No, but on the other hand I bet you do next time. I know I will. Unfortunately that's the way medicine's heading. We need to cover ourselves constantly. Doesn't mean I like it, though.'

'I guess.'

'Did she tell you about your interview?'

Lila looked up sharply. 'How do you know about that?'

'I'm sitting in on it.' He had the decency to wince. 'Sorry, Lila, Mr Hinkley's at a meeting on Wednesday. There was no way I could refuse without raising a few eyebrows.'

The tears were still threatening and Lila closed her eyes against them. It had been an emotional morning on top of an emotional weekend. All she wanted to do was sleep, to lie in bed and sleep for a whole week, but sleep would have to wait. There was Mum's bath, breakfast…

'Lila?' She could hear the concern in his voice. His hand brushed her arm then quickly he pulled away. They weren't lovers any more, they weren't even friends, just colleagues.

'Look, I could chuck a sicky on Wednesday.'

Lila shook her head. Opening her eyes, sparkling with tears, she managed a weak smile. 'It's just a job. I'm not going to collapse in a heap if I don't get it. And after Hester's little dressing-down, I'd say that's a foregone conclusion.'

'You don't have a problem with me being there?'

She even laughed. 'Of course I do, but I've a feeling if I'm going to carry on working here it's a problem I'm going to have to get used to. I'd better get home. Thanks for sticking up for me in there.'

'No worries.'

The air was thick with so many unspoken words.

'What I said on Saturday night—'

'You meant.' Lila finished for him.

'I did,' he agreed wearily. 'And I still do. But it's not that easy, is it?'

Declan was right. It wasn't that easy—*nothing* was easy. Sitting on her bed, Lila surveyed the piles of discarded clothes. She couldn't even decide what to wear for her interview. Decisions, changes, her world was full of them.

She'd seen the holiday brochures Shirley had hastily pushed under the sofa when she'd come downstairs. It didn't anger Lila—all it did was make her feel ever more guilty. Guilty that Ted and Shirley should have to think twice about enjoying their retirement. Guilty that she wished she could enjoy herself, too.

Decisions about her career. How could she take on an appointment with an even higher level of responsibility when she could barely cope with the demands of a full-time job, and that was with Shirley's and Ted's support? And as for a relationship…

Refusing to even go down that path, Lila stood up abruptly. OK, senior role, serious clothes. She wasn't exactly spoiled for choice but the camel-coloured suit was an old faithful. Perhaps the skirt was a tad too short, but if she wore some smart loafers and sheer stockings it would smarten the outfit up. Lila brushed her hair then started to coil it into the usual topknot for work. She stopped. Why not leave it down for once? A generous blob of hair serum and half an hour with the hairdryer saw her blonde waves eradicated, leaving instead a heavy sleek blonde curtain. And not for the first time since Declan had reappeared into her life, Lila took extra care with her make-up, delightedly rediscovering her cheekbones along the way.

Finally, as she stood facing the full-length mirror, a small grin tugging at her lips, she put her hands to each side.

'The exit signs are located here and here.' Not quite the gorgeous sleek thing of yesteryear but pretty close. Declan wouldn't know what had hit him.

Declan.

Was all the grooming, the extra effort for his benefit?

Throwing in a hairbrush, Lila snapped her handbag closed. Of course it wasn't. She was going to an interview, for heaven's sake. Anyone would have made an effort.

Still, she grudgingly admitted as she liberally sprayed her wrists and neck, the perfume was hardly for Hester's benefit.

Making her way down the stairs, Lila brushed off Shirley's flattering comment as she fed her sister her lunch. 'You look fabulous, darling, just like the Lila of old, doesn't she, Elizabeth?'

With a self-conscious smile Lila crossed the room. 'Hardly, but I thought I'd better make a bit of an effort, I've got a few brownie points against me where Hester's concerned. Here, let me give Mum her lunch. I've got a bit of time before I have to go.'

'I don't think pumpkin soup would go very well on that suit. Why don't you go while you've got the chance? Surprise that boss of yours by being early for once?'

'OK, then.' Kissing her mother, Lila turned to her aunt. 'Wish me luck?'

'You don't need luck, Lila, you'll get the job on your own merits. But I'll say it anyway—good luck, darling.' Putting down the bowl of soup, Shirley pulled her niece into a warm embrace. 'You're a good girl, Lila, you always were. We're all very proud of you whatever happens with the interview.'

Lila hugged her aunt back, closing her eyes as she did so. She knew Shirley meant well, but this interview had suddenly taken on monumental importance. She had to get this job, had to pull in some more money, there was no two ways about it. Today mattered.

'Come in, Nurse Bailey, and take a seat. Sorry to keep you waiting.' Hester gestured to the chair as Lila walked in. The wait in the staffroom had been unbearable. Self-conscious in her suit, Lila had made small talk with the other applicants, her despondency growing as she'd listened to their qualifications and experience. And not one of them looked as if they'd ever been late for anything in their lives. It was almost a relief to escape to Hester's office.

Only almost.

Declan gave a guarded smile as she sat down. He at least had the decency to look uncomfortable as she entered, but it did nothing to disguise the spark of admiration in his eyes when he saw her.

The chair Hester had hauled into the office for the interviews was way too low and instantly Lila regretted the short skirt, flashing rather too much stocking-clad thigh as she crossed her legs at the ankles.

'Well,' Hester began, her gaze flickering to Lila's legs; her lips pursed as if she were chewing on a lemon. 'It's always rather *difficult*, interviewing current staff members for a position. However, it's not only mandatory, it's also merited. Particularly for such a senior position. There are a couple of issues I'd like to address in a formal setting before we make our decision.'

'Of course.' The bright smile Lila forced belied the dive her stomach had taken.

At first Hester busied herself with the basics—salary, duties, responsibilities—but all too soon the conversation turned.

'My main concern, Nurse Bailey, is that you are an extremely popular staff member.'

Lila looked her senior directly in the eye. 'I would have thought that would have been an advantage.'

'In some instances, of course. However, in the position you're applying for there will be a need to discipline staff at times. Are you going to be able to do that?'

Lila took a deep breath. She had been expecting this question. As much as she wanted the job, there was no point in lying.

'If there's a problem I will most certainly address it, and when necessary take the matter further.'

'But are you prepared to treat your colleagues as colleagues and not friends?'

Lila glanced over at Declan, who was watching her closely. Almost imperceptibly he gave her a small nod of encouragement. It was the encouragement she needed.

'I don't see them as being exclusive of each other. I believe—strongly, in fact—that the team works better as friends.'

Lila paused, not for effect but to gather her thoughts. 'I know you and I don't agree on this, Hester. And I'm not saying that I'm right and you're wrong. We have different styles of management and in my case I work better and deal with staff issues better by being friends with my colleagues.'

'What if you caught a *friend* stealing?'

Heavens, Hester was such an optimist sometimes! Lila took a deep breath, physically forcing herself not to roll her eyes. 'Then, of course, I'd address it. Firstly it would depend on what was being stolen. Obviously drugs would cause me rather more concern than a couple of bandaids.'

Not the right answer! She watched as Hester's lips disappeared into her face. 'If everyone employed in the hospital stocked up their first-aid boxes courtesy of the hospital, where would that leave the budgets?'

'Taking anything is wrong, of course.' Lila added hastily before she continued her answer. 'First and foremost I'd try to find out the reasoning behind the stealing and what had driven them to do it, and on the basis of that information I'd make my decision as to the appropriate action.'

Hester looked far from mollified by her response, and Lila frantically tried to think of a more suitable answer but one that didn't compromise her beliefs.

'What would be your priority?' It was the first time Declan had spoken, and Lila looked over at him again quickly, her brow furrowing at his question. But, like a mist clearing, she realised the appropriate answer he was feeding her.

'My priority would always be the well-being of the patients and the safe running of the department. I would never compromise on that. I'm a nurse first.'

It was a good answer, or at the very least enough to set Hester shuffling the paperwork in front of her. 'Well, Nurse Bailey, I think we've covered everything. Doctor Haversham, is there anything else you'd like to ask?'

Lila relaxed back in her chair a fraction, glad the painfully embarrassing procedure was coming to an end.

A foolish mistake.

'With the other applicants we've discussed the impact such a demanding position might place on their personal lives…' Lila felt her shoulders stiffen as Declan continued, his face impassive. 'Or, more to the point, the demands their personal lives might have on this position. I'd like to hear from Lila if she's given this any thought.'

Hester's dismissive laughter should have come as

a relief. 'Oh, we don't have to worry about that with Nurse Bailey. She's footloose and fancy-free.'

Lines she'd never before seen suddenly darkened in Declan's forehead.

'But surely her mo—' The words died on his lips as he caught Lila's anguished look from across the table.

Licking her dry lips, Lila broke in quickly. 'As Hester pointed out, I don't have a husband or children. I'm more than able to cope with the demands of the job.'

'Then it seems that we've covered everything.' Hester's face twisted into an attempt at a smile. 'We've still got a few more applicants to interview, but hopefully we shan't keep you too long before we let you know the outcome.' Standing, she offered her hand. 'Thank you for your time, Nurse Bailey.'

'Sure.' The handshake was cursory, an obvious conclusion to the interview, but as Lila turned and offered her hand to Declan there was nothing perfunctionary about the hand that gripped hers.

Daring to look up, she saw the dart of confusion in his eyes, the dearth of questions, the utter despair.

Walking past the staffroom, it came as no surprise as he ran up behind her.

'Lila?' She heard the question in his voice but kept on walking.

'Lila, please. We need to talk.'

Turning slowly, she shook her head. 'There's nothing more to say.'

'There's plenty. Lila, they don't even know, do they?' When she didn't answer he continued, his voice thick with emotion, 'They don't know about your mother. You go on about friendship, about comradeship, and your own friends don't even know what's going on in your life.'

'I don't want to talk about it.' Hitching her bag up an inch on her shoulder, Lila made to go, but Declan wasn't finished.

'Well, I do.'

He was almost shouting.

Anxiously she cast a look around. 'You've got interviews,' she said. 'You can't just disappear.'

'It's lunchtime. Look, why don't we go to the canteen, grab something to eat and try to sort things out once and for all?'

'I have to get home, Declan.' His eyes stayed on her and she knew he wasn't going to give up without making a scene. 'Just for five minutes, then.'

The canteen was fairly quiet. Most of the lunchtime traffic had been and gone and they moved uncomfortably along the counter, pushing their trays without speaking. Lila put a limp-looking salad on her tray and a cup of coffee. Declan chose a giant chocolate-chip cookie and a huge half-litre bottle of cola. 'I'm here till five.' He shrugged as he caught her surreptitiously watching him pile up his tray. 'I need the energy boost.'

They found a table in the corner and busied themselves opening boxes and wrappers, spooning in sugar—anything other than look at each other.

It was Declan who broke the uneasy silence.

'I'm worried about you, Lila.'

When she didn't respond he continued, 'I know until a couple of weeks ago I hadn't seen you in ages, I know I'm not part of your life any more, but it doesn't stop me from being concerned.'

'There's nothing to be concerned about.'

'You've changed, Lila.'

She gave a hollow laugh. 'I seem to rather clearly remember you telling me that the problem was that I hadn't changed. I was still the immature spoilt brat you knew of old.'

'Please, Lila, I didn't come here to row.'

'Me neither.' Taking a sip of her coffee, Lila leant back in her chair. 'So in what way have I changed?'

'That's what I've been trying to work out, but I can't put my finger on it. You still like a laugh, you're fun to work with, you're actually a great nurse, the department really lifts when you're in charge—'

'But.' He looked up sharply at her interruption. 'I'm assuming there is one?'

'Your sparkle seems to have gone.' He grimaced

slightly as he said it. 'If that sounds really tacky I'm sorry, it's the best I can do.'

'Declan.' With a sigh Lila finally looked up at him. 'When we used to go out I was in my early twenties, I had a fantastic job, no responsibilities. My biggest decision was what colour lipstick to wear. It was pretty easy to sparkle then. But even then you never saw me at work, you just saw the lighter side of me. You're seeing me now in charge of five staff and whatever patient comes through the hospital doors, I've got a sick mother, I'm eight years older...'

'All of which I've taken into consideration, but it still doesn't stop me from worrying.' He hesitated before tentatively continuing, 'Just how sick is Elizabeth?'

'Why?' Lila answered rudely. 'Were you planning on sending a get-well card?' He didn't answer. In fact, he didn't say anything, his question still hovering unanswered between them.

'She's not well at all,' Lila responded finally.

'Is she very confused? I mean, do you have to watch her all the time?'

Lila shook her head. 'She's a bit beyond that,' she admitted reluctantly.

'How far beyond?'

Her eyes travelled around the bland canteen, searching for a diversion.

'Do you get any help?'

Her blue eyes finally met his, but only briefly. 'Ted and Shirley have been great.'

'I meant professional help. The district nursing service, carer support, that sort of thing.'

She didn't like the way the conversation was heading. Didn't like the probing nature of his questions. The truth, however rosily painted, could only lead to one conclusion. Elizabeth Bailey should be in a home.

Pushing away her uneaten salad, Lila picked her bag up from the floor. 'Why the sudden concern about my mother, Declan? We're not a couple. You made it clear the other night that you're through worrying about me...'

'We may not be a couple but we are colleagues. For heaven's sake, Lila, we've got a few contacts between us. Maybe Yvonne could take a look...'

'No.' The word came out too loudly and a couple of curious faces turned in their direction. Flushing slightly, Lila lowered her voice. 'It's not as if you and Mum even liked each other. Why should things change now?'

'That's it, isn't it?' His eyes flashed angrily. 'That's the whole root of it.'

'What?' Lila shook her head, bemused, as he continued.

'The fact your mother never did like me. It never sat right with you, did it?'

Lila shrugged then checked herself, remembering how much she hated that response in him.

'No matter what I did, it was never quite good enough, was it? And you believed her when she said I wasn't any good for you. You spent the whole of our relationship waiting for me to let you down, waiting for your mother to be proved right...'

'I did not,' Lila retorted furiously.

'Yes, Lila, you did.' Declan pushed his own plate away. 'And the second I failed some imaginary test, the second I didn't respond accordingly, you dumped me.'

For a second she thought he was going to walk out but he didn't. Instead, Declan closed his eyes for a second, shaking his head slightly as if clearing his thoughts. 'We didn't come here for this,' he said slowly, his voice even now. 'Going over and over the past doesn't solve anything. What we have to deal with is the here and now. How we're going to work together, how we're going to be colleagues and maybe one day friends even. But I can't wave some magic wand and stop worrying about you, not notice the changes in you. And if I can help then I will.'

'You can't, Declan. And I'm not saying that because it's you. No one can help. It's my problem. Mum probably *should* be in a nursing home but I

just can't do that to her. It's not going to go on for
ever, I know she's not going to be around for much
longer. I just want to do the right thing by her for
however long she's got left.' Lila's eyes misted over.
'Maybe you're right. Maybe I did put too much cre-
dence in what Mum said about you. Mum was let
down badly when Dad left, and in some way I guess
her distrust of men affected me, but—'

'Let's not go there, Lila.' Declan's voice was suddenly gruff. 'I really don't want to argue any more.
Will you at least think about talking to Yvonne?
Surely some help is better than none.' He glanced
down at her hands as she poured yet another pile of
sugar onto her spoon and slowly dunked it her coffee.
'Why won't you let us help you, Lila?'

As her spoon idly drifted to the sugar bowl again
he caught her hand.

'Why, Lila? What are you scared of?'

The flash of tears in her eyes, the tension lines that
pursed her lips tore through Declan.

'You want to know what I'm scared of?' Her
choking voice was almost a whisper as she gripped
his hand tightly, her blue eyes lifting to meet his
own. 'I'm so scared that when the district nurse
comes, when the physio and the social workers all
descend and come to the natural conclusion as to
where Mum should be…I'm scared that I'll give in
and agree. I'm scared that the light at the end of the

tunnel will be so bloody bright I'll cover my eyes and do the "sensible" thing. Scared that the chance of actually having my life back will be too hard to turn down.'

Lila didn't swear, ever.

Until now.

'Bloody' was hardly big league, but to hear the expletive come from her lips he knew the depth of Lila's despair, knew the agony behind her words.

'I want to be there for you,' he rasped. 'Please, Lila, let's sort this out together. Let me help you.'

She felt as if she'd been in prison for years, that the jailer was standing waving a shiny key, offering her a glimpse of life outside.

And she was tempted, so tempted to slip her hand between the bars and grab that key, grab her chance of escape. But that would mean running away—away from the responsibilities, away from the promise she'd made to care for her mother.

Declan might care, might think he could help, but how could he possibly know what he would be letting himself in for? Some day—not tomorrow, next week or next month even. Some day in the future there would be a party or a holiday or any tiny thing that would force the issue, force her to choose.

It took a superhuman effort to shake her head, to pull her hand back between the bars into the safety of her self-imposed jail.

'All I want from you, Declan, is to forget what you know. I need your assurance that no one at work will find out how things are for me at home.'

'And that's all you want?'

'That's it.' Lila stood up.

'Lila, please, there's something I need to say.'

With a sigh she sat down again, her bag still over her shoulder, ready to leave at any moment.

'I'm not doing this because I want to get back with you.'

Her eyes lifted to his and he saw a flicker of confusion there.

'I'm doing this because we work together, because of what we used to feel. As good as the other night was, it taught me one thing. We really are over. We don't love each other, and it's good that we both finally realise it. Now at last we can move on, stop feeling awkward around each other.' He gave a small laugh as she fought to hold herself together. 'And to prove my point, I'm even thinking of asking Yvonne out. I've never really looked at her before in that way but, well, she's nice, and she seems to like me. It's enough to be going on with.'

When Lila didn't answer he carried on, his voice positive, assured. 'Lila, we're a couple of exes who happen to work together. It's no crime we don't love each other. There just wasn't enough there to sustain a relationship. But a friendship? Well, I think even we could manage that, a real one this time, though. Not the half-hearted effort of a couple of weeks ago.'

He gave a small smile and she managed a watery one back.

She had been waiting to rebuff him, to politely refuse his requests for another try. Not this!

Never this.

He was over her, finally and completely over her. And it hurt like hell.

'Friends help each other,' he said softly.

She couldn't look at him, terrified he would read the utter despair in her eyes.

'Will you let me ask Yvonne?'

'You don't need my permission to date her.'

He gave her a nonplussed look. 'I meant about arranging some services for your mum.'

Ouch! A deep blush started to spread upwards from her neck. 'I really need to get home.'

'Lila, at least say that you'll think about it.'

'I'll think about it,' she agreed finally, and with a small smile walked purposefully out of the canteen, managing to keep her composure along the endless corridor to the staff exit. Waving cheerfully at a couple of familiar faces, she finally made it to the solitude of her car.

Only when she was safely inside, with the ignition turned on and the radio blaring, did Lila let the tears start.

CHAPTER SEVEN

IT WAS a relief the department was busy that night. Too busy for Lila to think about her own problems and too busy for the awareness that usually descended upon her whenever Declan was around.

'I've got Ambulance Control on the line, Lila,' Sue called as Lila dashed past. 'They want to speak to whoever's in charge.'

'Thanks, Sue.' Tucking the telephone between her shoulder and ear, she handed Sue a plastic dish. 'Cubicle three feels nauseous. Can you give her this? Declan's written her up for some Maxalon if you get a moment.' She returned her attention to the phone. 'Nurse Bailey here.'

'Nurse, we're bringing in a forty-five-year-old female. Fell from a horse. Possible loss of consciousness and a left ankle injury.'

Lila frowned at the telephone. Why on earth were they alerting her about a simple head injury?

'The problem is that the patient concerned is your unit manager.'

'Hester!'

'That's right. She was very reluctant to come in, but she needs stitching and she's slightly disorientated and agitated. The paramedics have managed to persuade her to come, but I thought we should warn you.'

'Thanks so much.'

Poor Hester. As much as Lila didn't like the woman, she meant her no harm. Arriving in your own department as a patient was embarrassing to say the least. Protocol bound the paramedics to bring all patients to the nearest emergency department. The least Lila could do was ensure Hester's privacy as much as possible and try to keep the amount of staff that dealt with her to the minimum.

'Can I do anything to help?' Vera's rouged cheeks and reddened lips seemed ridiculously out of place with her shabby jacket and unkempt hair. 'You look ever so busy.'

'We are tonight, Vera.' Lila spoke kindly. 'But the doctor *will* take a look at your leg just as soon as the department quietens down.'

'Oh, that's all right, Lila, you know I don't mind waiting. It's just I feel so useless sitting there, doing nothing. Surely there must be something I can do?'

The most helpful thing Vera could do right now was take a seat and be quiet and a lot of staff would have told her to do just that, but it wasn't in Lila's nature. It would also have been entirely counter-productive as unless Vera was given something to occupy her, the incessant pleas to help would only increase.

Grabbing a pile of dusters and bin liners, Lila handed them to a beaming Vera. 'These have to be folded, Vera. I hate to ask but we really are busy.'

'I'd be happy to.' Her toothless smile was as wide as her face.

'But very neatly, mind,' Lila said seriously. 'Or my boss will be very angry. It's going to take you a while, Vera. Are you sure you don't mind?'

'Not a bit. I'm just glad to be some help to you all. I know how hard you all work.' And taking the pile of dusters and bin liners, she walked importantly off to the waiting room.

Happy Vera was settled, Lila set about preparing a cubicle for Hester. She'd have a fit if she saw Vera handling the hospital supplies, but it was only a pile of dusters and bin liners after all. Poor old girl. After Hester's clamp-down she couldn't even give Vera a breakfast in the morning. Still, Hester couldn't stop her giving Vera a cup of tea and some biscuits and cake from the night staff's own stash.

The paramedics' warning had been spot on. Hester was indeed less than happy to be a patient, although one look at her cut and swollen face left Lila in no doubt that she needed medical intervention. Ushering the paramedics into cubicle one, she smiled warmly at her senior.

'Hi, Hester, we'll just get you over on to the trolley and make you a bit more comfortable.'

'I can manage fine myself.' Pushing away Lila's helping hands, she attempted to sit herself up, only to stifle a scream as she collapsed unwillingly back onto the stretcher.

'Steady there, love.' The paramedic's kind words only inflamed Hester further.

'I'm not your "love". Now, if you'll leave me be for two minutes you'll realise that I can manage fine myself.'

But her second attempt at moving proved equally futile, and with a yelp of pain and frustration Hester lay defeated against the pillow.

'Perhaps if I hold your ankle, you could lift yourself over,' Lila suggested, her voice steady and firm.

A small hint of a nod deemed that Hester was at least prepared to finally accept some assistance.

Her ankle was grotesquely swollen and cold but, given that she had been outside for some hours, that could be more due to exposure than lack of circulation and Lila would make a more careful assessment once her patient was safely on the trolley. Concentrating on holding the leg steady as Hester painfully inched her way over, Lila noticed that Hester quickly covered herself with the blanket.

'Thanks, guys.' She noticed the wide-eyed look the paramedic gave her, which indicated there was more to be said. Covering Hester with a further blanket, Lila excused herself and slipped outside.

'I think she's had a bit of an accident, and not the falling-off-your-horse kind.'

Lila grinned at the paramedic's description.

'Of course she won't admit it but, given that she was out there for four or five hours, it's hardly surprising. We offered to cut her trousers off and put her into a gown but she wouldn't have a bar of it. Not the sunniest person, your boss, is she?'

Lila feigned surprise. 'I don't know what you're talking about. She's an absolute sweetheart.'

'Nurse Bailey!' The angry shout from the cubicle made them all grin. 'Told you,' she said with a wry grin. 'I'll catch you later.

'Hester, I'm just going to do your obs and have a look at your ankle then I'll get you into a gown and Declan will come and take a look at you. I've spoken to him already and once he's checked you're stable he'll ring Mr Hinkley and have him come in and check you out.'

Calling a consultant in from home for such a minor injury wasn't necessary, more a courtesy extended as Hester was the manager of the unit.

'I don't want Mr Hinkley brought in. I just want some strapping on my ankle. Hopefully by then my husband will be here to take me home.'

'Hester, please, you know your ankle needs more

than a bit of strapping. Now, can I do your observations?'

With a heavy sigh Hester leant back on the pillows. 'If you must.'

Her observations were all within normal limits, except a slightly low temperature. Checking her foot, Lila was pleased to see that Hester could move her toes and when pushed gently the colour soon returned, showing she had good circulation to the affected area. A nasty gash on her forehead required a few stitches. The paramedic had said that she'd seemed disorientated but that didn't appear evident now. As for agitation, Lila guessed it had rather more to do with the embarrassment of finding herself in the department, particularly if she'd had an 'accident'.

'What happened, Hester?'

'I'm sure the ambulancemen told you.'

'Of course, but I need to hear it from you.'

'I was riding,' she said grudgingly. 'And obviously I came off.'

'Why?' Lila pressed, though her question visibly irritated Hester. It was important to ascertain whether some event, such as a faint or convulsion, had caused her fall or if it had been a straightforward accident.

'Trigger just started suddenly—something must have scared him—and then he threw me. And, yes,' she snapped, 'I remember everything. I wasn't knocked out.'

Lila didn't say anything for a moment, just busied herself placing some sterile gauze over the laceration on Hester's forehead. 'You're sure about that?'

'Maybe I was knocked out for a couple of seconds, but no longer,' Hester admitted. 'But Trigger was still fretting when I came to, so it really wasn't for long. Poor thing.' Lila watched as Hester's face softened. 'He stayed by me the whole time, whinnying and worried. He's such a brave horse. I'll be sure and give him an extra treat for breakfast.'

Lila bit back a smart reply as she thought of dear old Vera folding dusters, desperate to help. Hester would rather the horses were fed than her patients.

'Good.' Lila wrote down her observations on the back of the casualty card. 'Let's get you into a gown.'

In a second the barriers that had come down slightly were erected again. 'I don't need a gown. Now, will you, please, leave me alone!'

Lila knew that for once Hester's sharp words weren't personal. Lila saw Hester for what she was, a strongly proud woman, embarrassed with absolutely no need to be. They were both nurses, both women, yet Lila knew she would have felt the same. She thought for a moment how to play this, how she would feel if it were her lying there and her colleagues needed to have instant access to her body at such a vulnerable time.

'Hester, I know this must be difficult for you,' Lila said gently. 'It is for me, too.'

Hester looked up sharply at Lila's admission.

'I know how I'd feel if I'd been lying out on a field somewhere for five hours and Declan Haversham had to come in and examine me.'

The tiny grin on Hester's face told Lila she was on the right track. 'A girl's got her pride. Why don't I get you a bowl and you can have a wash? I'll find you a comb and you can put on a gown. I can help you off with your jodhpurs and top and then I'll leave you.'

Hester nodded. 'Thank you. It's just that while I was lying there, while I was waiting to be found, there was nothing I could do. I had—'

Lila patted her arm. 'Leave it to me.'

When Lila returned with a bowl and towels she gave Hester a smile. 'I'm sure these aren't to your taste but I ordered them from Sue's lingerie party. They've been in my locker.' She handed Hester the underwear, still in its Cellophane.

'I'll pay you.'

Lila winked. 'Take it as a first payment on the bandages and breakfasts.'

'And you won't write it down on my casualty card.' She watched as Lila frowned. It could be relevant. 'Of course, you'll have to let the doctor know but, Nurse Bailey, you know as well as I do that everyone who comes in contact with my casualty card will be sure to have a good read.'

Lila nodded. Hester had a point. Just the fact she now knew Hester's age was more personal detail than five years in the department had given her.

'I wouldn't worry, Hester.' Lila couldn't resist the dig. 'When do I get a chance to document things properly? You know yourself how bad I am at that.'

Once cleaned up and in a crisp lemon gown, Hester was the perfect patient, answering Declan's questions politely, gratefully accepting the painkilling injection Lila gave her.

Once she was safely wheeled off to X-Ray, with her rather nervous-looking husband hurrying behind, Declan gave Lila a grin.

'I've rung Mr Hinkley and he's on his way, I know she said not to but I'm sure it's expected really. He'll have a look at her X-rays and make a few polite noises. Hopefully that will appease her. She should really be admitted overnight for neuro obs.'

'Not a chance.' Lila shook her head. 'The obs ward's full and there's no way you'll persuade her to go up to a ward. You know how difficult she can be.'

'What if she stays down here on a trolley? You could do her obs and I'll check her over before the day staff arrive and hopefully she'll be able to go home. It would save her the embarrassment of a full admission.'

'I don't have a problem with it, so long as Hester doesn't moan when she audits the trolley times.'

Declan laughed. 'I'm sure she will. Still, there's obviously more to Hester than meets the eye.'

'In what way?' Lila found herself smiling as Declan started to laugh.

'Well, not that I've ever pictured Hester in her undies but, if pushed, black velvet wouldn't have been the image I'd have come up with.'

Thumping him on the arm, Lila laughed as she blushed. He probably knew the undies were hers—after all, she had told him about Hester's accident. Still, it was a good reason for a giggle.

And heaven knew, they needed it. The tension between them recently had been almost unbearable.

'Over here a minute, Lila.' Sue's voice had a note of urgency in it that snapped Lila to attention. Helping Sue with the trolley she was pushing, she guided it into Resus, looking at the flushed child lying drowsily on it.

'What's the problem?'

'She was just lining up with her parents in the waiting room and the triage nurse asked me to see her straight away. Flu-like symptoms, pain in the legs, reluctant to walk. I've told her parents to wait in the interview room.'

'What's her temp?' Declan's deep voice had an edge of concern as he pulled his stethoscope from around his neck and Lila put the tympanic thermometer into the child's ear.

'Thirty-nine.'

Declan started his examination as Lila undressed the little girl. Pulling off the child's jeans, Lila felt her throat tighten. 'Declan.' The note in her voice was enough to immediately get his attention. Looking down to where she was pointing, Lila watched his brow furrow as he saw the insidious purple rash appearing on Amy's legs.

'Sue,' Lila called. 'Page Paediatrics now. Do you want me to set up for a lumbar puncture?' she added, addressing Declan.

He shook his head, concentrating on trying to find a vein so he could insert an intravenous bung—no mean feat in a child as sick as this. 'Not yet. I'll take some blood off now and then let's get some antibiotics and fluids into her, stat. Put on some oxygen.'

As Lila did so he looked up briefly. 'Do we have a name?'

Peeling the name band off the top of the casualty card, Lila wrapped it around the child's limp wrist. 'Amy Phillips.'

He stopped for a second. Although time was of

the essence, so was reassuring the patient, however sick.

'Amy, my name's Declan. I'm a doctor. You're just going to feel a small scratch in your hand and then I'll be able to give you some medicines that will make you feel better soon.'

As Lila attached the intravenous infusion, Sue arrived back, breathless. 'Paeds are stuck with a collapsed child on the ward, the anaesthetist too.'

'What the hell is this, then?' Declan retorted sharply, and Lila could hear the tension in his voice.

'Sue.' Lila's voice was calm and assured. 'Tell Switchboard to page the paediatric consultant at home. Declan or I will speak with him. Tell them also to page the second-on paediatricians. Then ring ICU and check if they've got a paediatric bed.' She glanced over at Declan, who was administrating the intravenous antibiotics. 'Do you want the second anaesthetist?'

'Yep. Get these bloods off stat and tell the lab I want the results yesterday.'

'Sure.'

The rash seemed to be darkening with lightning speed. A huge infection was literally overwhelming the little girl as they spoke, and the paediatricians were involved with another sick child.

Sue returned, and with one look at her anxious face Lila knew more trouble was coming.

'The paramedics just alerted us. They're at a house fire, four children inside and one adult. Two firefighters are suffering from smoke inhalation.'

Lila felt her heart plummet for a second. Catching Declan's eyes for a second, she knew he felt it too.

This was the how quickly the wind on the front line could suddenly turn.

This was night duty in Emergency.

'How long till they get here?'

'Ten minutes.'

Amy was desperately ill, they had a department full of sick people, but in just ten short minutes four children and three adults were going to arrive, possibly all desperately ill.

Lila had to think on her feet. There was a thin line in Emergency between overreacting and calling a major incident or waiting to see how the events unfolded and running the risk of calling it too late.

'Fast-page the nurse supervisor. I want the wards rung and told to come immediately and get the patients that are assigned to them.'

'Right.'

'Get the other staff down to Resus.'

The paediatric emergency trolley had already been opened for Amy and quickly Lila filled kidney dishes with intravenous bungs, alcohol swabs, paediatric airways.

Any patient that could be was moved out of the

area in an attempt to clear some room. As the wail of sirens heralded the arrival of the first ambulance, Lila took the phone from Sue.

'Dr Harper here.'

Lila felt a wave of relief wash over her. Gerard Harper wasn't only a brilliant paediatrician, he was also a nice man, happy to share a coffee and a chat. At least it wasn't a virtual stranger on the other end of the line. 'Gerard, it's Lila Bailey here—I'm the nurse in charge of Emergency tonight. We have a five-year-old with suspected meningococcal disease and also an alert from the paramedics of an attempt to rescue four children from a house fire.'

'I'm on my way, Lila. I'll ring a couple of colleagues on my mobile.'

Lila didn't bother to say thank you. There truly wasn't time.

Mr Hinkley arrived with the first ambulance and Lila quickly briefed him. Mercifully the child the paramedics were dashing in with was crying loudly, a good sign by any standards.

'Nurse Bailey, what on earth's going on? I heard all the emergency pages.' Hester's face was anxious as she struggled to sit up.

Even though Hester was a patient, she was still the unit manager. The potential gravity of the situation would have made Lila consider ringing her boss even if she'd been at home, so Lila told her, watching as Hester's eyes widened.

'Are you calling more staff in?'

'Not at this stage.' Lila saw the flash of doubt in Hester's expression. 'Mr Hinkley was already here to see you and Gerard Harper is on his way to see a child with suspected meningococcal disease. I've spoken to him on his mobile and he's going to alert some colleagues. I've also got the nurse supervisor plus an ICU nurse coming down.'

'I should be out there. Nurse Bailey, get me off this trolley and into a wheelchair.' For a second the sight of Vera flashed through Lila's mind, desperate to be of some assistance but getting in the way.

'Hester, you've got a head injury and a fractured ankle. You're a patient, *my* patient. The best thing you can do is rest quietly and let me get on with my job. I promise if I need advice you'll be the first person I come to.'

Hester looked at her suspiciously. 'You promise?'

Lila nodded. 'Look, Hester, I have to go.' As she left she turned briefly. 'But I'm really glad you're here.'

The strangest thing was, she was actually speaking the truth.

A blue light was flashing past the windows of Resus. Dashing out to the ambulance bay, the cool night air hit Lila. Running, she pulled open the rear ambulance door, praying that the sight that would greet her would be another crying child.

It wasn't.

The pink face of the five-year-old girl belied how sick she was. Carbon monoxide, a silent killer, caused the skin to turn a false, healthy-looking pink.

Lila took over the cardiac massage as the paramedics raced the trolley into the resuscitation room.

'Pulled out of the front bedroom, no pulse or respiratory effort, we've been working on her for fourteen minutes now.' A paramedic reeled off the drugs the child had been given. They had already intubated the little girl and the anaesthetist took over, pushing the oxygen gently but rapidly into the child in an effort to increase her oxygen concentration.

'There's another ambulance working on child number three at the scene. She was flat when they pulled her out but I just heard from Ambulance Control that she seems to be picking up.'

Lila nodded, not looking up as she carried on the necessary conversation. It was imperative they knew what else to expect, but she continued with the cardiac massage. 'I thought there were four children.'

The paramedic nodded grimly. 'The firefighters are still searching.'

'What about the parents?' Declan's voice sounded strangely hoarse as he pushed some drugs into the intravenous line that had been inserted into the child's hand. No one liked dealing with such sick children and Lila knew he was devastated by the turn of events that had seen a usual busy night turn into a disaster for one family and an emotional rollercoaster for all the emergency staff involved.

'Dad's away on business, Mum's got facial and hand burns but she won't leave till we find the fourth child. The police are contacting the father now, poor guy. Imagine picking up the telephone and hearing about this.'

'How old is the child that's missing?'

'Two.' He turned and made his way down the corridor. Back to the ambulance, back to the scene to do whatever had to be done.

There was no goodbye. No cheery 'Catch you later'.

Two.

The tiny number said it all.

CHAPTER EIGHT

'STOP the massage.' Declan raised one hand as he watched the cardiac monitor. The other hand was placed on the child's neck, his eyes, his ears, his fingers straining to acknowledge even the tiniest sign of life in this precious young child.

Lila rested back on her heels. Long ago she had abandoned standing on the floor as she'd given cardiac massage. Up on the trolley, astride the patient, the massage was more effective. On a small child like this it was important not to apply too much force, but in prolonged resuscitations such as this one it was tiring work. It was the fourth time Declan had told her to stop, the fourth time they'd held their breaths as they'd willed the drugs, the massage, the utter energy they'd been expending to somehow do its magic and work.

They didn't say anything—there was no need. But as the flat line on the monitor suddenly blipped, then blipped again, the flickering of a rhythm as it picked up the electrical impulses in the child's heart, she heard Declan exhale and realised he'd been holding his breath also.

'Come on, baby,' he urged. 'Come on.' As if hearing the urgency in his voice, the rhythm picked up, slow and tentative at first but gaining in momentum until a steady pulse could not only be seen but palpated in her neck and her wrists.

But this was only the first step. The real test came later. They might have got her heart beating again, but there was still a long way to go. Now she needed to breathe unaided, to show a sign that her brain hadn't been damaged. There was no way of knowing how long she had been down before the firefighters had got to her.

Her fixed, dilated pupils were an ominous sign of brain damage but, as Declan optimistically pointed out, the drugs she had been given at the scene of the fire and again in Resus would cause that also.

'I'll keep hyperventilating her,' the anaesthetist said as the latest blood-gas results were thrust at him. 'Blow off some of this carbon monoxide. She should have some mannitol as well—there's bound to be some cerebral oedema. Apart from that, it's wait and see.'

'Have you got a bed?'

The anaesthetist shook his head. 'We're getting Amy up there. I've got a patient that can be moved in the morning but it will mean keeping this little lady down here till then.'

Lila chewed her lip. 'I'll have to see—we're so busy. If not, the supervisor will have to do a ring around the other hospitals and see where there's a bed.'

'No worries,' the anaesthetist said with an easy smile. 'Let me know what happens. I'm not going anywhere for the moment.'

'How's Amy?' Lila asked as Sue made her way in.

Sue's grimace spoke volumes. 'Not the best. They've intubated her and I'm going to get her up to ICU now. Declan's in with her parents. Any news on the fourth child?'

Lila shook her head. 'The nurse supervisor will take Amy up for you. Can you set up this bed for child three? They've alerted us to say she's on the way now, though happily this one's breathing. Once you've got the bed set up, help the anaesthetist with child two. I'd better go out—the firefighters are starting to trickle in.'

She stood in the corridor, directing traffic for a moment. Catching sight of Hester's stricken face, Lila popped her head in.

'It's all under control, Hester.'

'All the children accounted for?'

Lila shook her head. 'All bar one. The firefighters are still looking.'

'No doubt they'll be in as patients next. Those guys never give up. Why don't you page the medics? They can take over the firefighters' care.'

'Done.'

Hester nodded. 'I feel so useless, lying here,' she admitted.

Lila gave a tight smile. 'We all feel like that, Hester, we all do.'

If Hester had been a reluctant patient, the firefighters were even worse. Desperate to get back to the scene, the emergency department was the last place they wanted to be.

Not when a two-year-old child was missing.

Assessing them was made harder by the layers of heavy clothing and apparatus, and their soot-blackened faces.

'You need oxygen and a chest X-ray,' Lila said firmly to Bruce Thomson, a young firefighter who struggled to get off the trolley.

'I ought to get back there.'

'You can't,' Lila said, exasperated. Flashing a torch up his nose, she saw the singed hairs which indicated his breathing passages could be burnt.

'She's right.' Declan came in behind her. His white coat was practically black, his hair was tousled and a streak of soot where he'd wiped his brow made him look as if he'd been out fighting the fire himself. Glancing at the casualty card, he shook Bruce's hand.

'Have you got kids, Bruce?'

'Yeah, one. He's the same age as the little tacker that's missing.'

'And, God forbid, if you were in these parents' position, would you want a firefighter with smoke inhalation on the scene? Wouldn't you rather the guys were looking for your child rather than looking out for their colleague?'

'I guess.'

She left them to it, grateful for Declan's tact and insight, grateful to all her staff for coping so well.

A tear-stained face greeted her as she pulled back the curtain. 'I want to help…' Vera was tearful, agitated. The unfolding events would have been especially traumatic for her, given her fragile mental state.

'Vera, please.' Lila heard the impatience in her own voice and immediately checked herself and changed track. 'There's really nothing you can do,' she finished gently.

'But the children, those poor babies…'

'We're looking after them.'

But Vera wasn't going to be mollified. 'I have to help, there must be something I can do, something I can do to help the babies…' It was the last thing Lila needed on top of everything else and she ran an exasperated hand, still dirtied with ash from the firefighter, through her long hair, trying to work out what on earth she was going to do with Vera.

'I could use a cuppa, Vera.' Declan's casual tone was a sharp contrast to Vera's. 'In fact, I'm sure all of the staff will be needing some refreshments fairly soon. Perhaps you could help with that later. I know the paramedics and firemen will be gasping.'

'And that will help?'

Declan grinned, his eyes crinkling in that, oh, so familiar fashion. 'Course it will, Vera. You know the saying that an army marches on its stomach. When things quieten down we'll let you know and you can make us all a cuppa. For now, though, if you take a seat we can get on.'

'You be sure and call me…'

'We will.'

Lila watched as Vera made her way towards the waiting room. 'Thanks for that. It's probably my fault in the first place for letting her hang around, but she's never got in the way before.'

Declan shrugged, only this time it didn't annoy her. If anything, there was an endearing nonchalance about him. 'She's not in the way now, just concerned. Everyone is.'

'Tell me about it. I've got Vera wanting to assist in Resus, Hester climbing off the gurney and firemen trying to escape.'

Declan laughed at her description. 'People just want to help. We've done all right, though. In fact, I think we've done a bloody good job.'

'We haven't finished yet,' Lila groaned. 'Now we've got the backlog to deal with.'

The trim phone was ringing shrilly, making them both jump.

'The backlog will have to wait,' Declan said pointedly as she picked up the phone, watching her face as she took Ambulance Control's message. 'What is it?'

'They're bringing the two-year-old in.' He saw the sparkle of tears glistening in her blue eyes.

'Bad?'

'No.' Her face broke into a wobbly grin. 'He's screaming the place down. Apparently he'd got out through the back laundry and climbed into a shed. They were just letting us know so we could stand down the paediatric Resus bed. He just needs to be checked over.'

'See?' Declan's face lit up at the unexpected happy news. 'Good things do happen, even when there seems no hope.'

Lila pulled a face. 'Don't go getting all philosophical on me, Declan. There's also two more firefighters coming in and the mother. The night's young yet.'

'Ah, this is the life.' Declan pulled off his tie and accepted a mug of coffee from Jez, carefully poured by Vera. 'How do you do it, Lila? You've got the surgical resident doing a drink round here.'

Lila took a grateful sip of her steaming drink.

'Teamwork. Jez, like every other mortal in the department, wanted to help, so Sue suggested he take Vera around. At least there was less chance with Jez of the nil-by-mouth patients getting a drink.' Lila winked at Sue. 'Looks like you've got a sweetheart there, Sue.'

'Don't I know it! Thank heaven you never came back to claim your drink.'

The less said about that the better! 'Can you believe how good the patients in the waiting room have been? Normally they'd be singing ''Why Are We Waiting?'' by now and tearing the place to bits.'

Declan shook his head. 'People are good really. A cup of coffee and an explanation work wonders.'

Draining her coffee, Lila stood up. 'Well, the coffee certainly does. I'd better go and do the Horse's obs.'

'With a bit of luck we'll be able to let her out of the stable by the morning.' Sue laughed loudly at her own joke.

There was a slightly manic edge to the conversation. The clock was edging towards six a.m. and the department was still full, yet for the first time on this shift there was no one critically ill, no one's life hanging in the balance. There was finally a chance for a quick drink and the zany type of debriefing emergency staff did only too well.

It was a slightly nervous Lila who made way for Vera to come out of Hester's cubicle.

'Sorry, Hester.' Lila gave her boss an apologetic smile. 'Vera wanted so badly to help, so I let her make the patients and staff a drink. Jez took her around, though,' Lila added hastily. 'None of the patients were compromised.'

'I'm sure they weren't. And the coffee was very welcome, too, I hasten to add.' Hester replaced her cup in its saucer. 'Vera was just telling me she used to get breakfast here until "the blooming boss" clamped down.'

Lila's already flushed cheeks grew even pinker.

'So, am I right in assuming that that's the reason for the increase in breakfast orders when you're in charge, Nurse Bailey?'

There was no point in lying. She'd been well and truly caught. 'I don't do it all the time, just for a few of the regulars that come in now and then to have their ulcers dressed or get their antibiotics, that type of thing. It seems such a shame to send them off hungry so sometimes I order breakfast for them.'

'Sometimes!' The irony in Hester's voice was blatant.

'Well, maybe a bit more than that sometimes.'

'Nurse Bailey, we're not a drop-in centre, we can't cater for every homeless person, as much as we'd like to.'

'I know,' Lila admitted, scuffing the floor with her foot.

'But I can't see that the occasional meal every now and then could do any harm. Perhaps, if it's not too late, you should ring the kitchen and order Vera a breakfast this morning. After all, she really has been a big help.'

Lila looked up sharply, unable to believe what she was hearing. 'She has, hasn't she?'

Hester nodded. 'But, Nurse Bailey, please, listen to me for a moment before you rush off. If you make a habit of it, providing food and blankets and shelter, people like Vera will come to expect it, depend on it even. Before you know it we'll have more people than we can deal with and nobody can benefit from a situation like that. There are services that provide meals for the homeless—we're an emergency unit. However, I do agree that now and then a bit of charity is merited. I'll leave it to you, Nurse, to make that call.'

'Thanks, Hester.' Lila found she was smiling genuinely at her boss for the first time in her memory. Declan's image of Hester in black velvet helped just a touch, though! 'Your obs are fine. No doubt Declan will give you your marching orders now.'

'Well, if he doesn't, I'm off anyway. I'll take a couple of days off but I'll be back soon enough.' For the first time ever Hester looked unsure of herself.

Lila watched as she pleated the blanket between her fingers. 'You did very well last night under difficult circumstances. It can't have been easy.'

'It wasn't.' Lila gave her boss a cheeky grin. 'My one major incident and I've got the unit manager with a ringside seat. That horse of yours must have had a sixth sense you needed to be at work.'

'Poor Trigger, he must have got such a fright. I can't wait to get home and see for myself how he's doing. He must be feeling awful right now.'

Lila rolled her eyes as she left the cubicle.

One day...*one day* Hester's voice was going to soften when she spoke about a human, and the whole department would stop dead in its tracks. Hester had missed her vocation in life—she really would have done better as a veterinary nurse!

Shirley took the news well that Lila was going to be late. The handover took for ever and a lot of time was spent on the telephone, arranging agency staff and extra cover to cope with the previous night's backlog as well as Hester's temporary absence. Still, as Lila made her way up the corridor towards the car park she couldn't resist popping into Intensive Care. As tired as Lila was, there was a method in her madness, for if she didn't see how the children were for herself she knew she would never get to sleep.

Part of the attraction of Emergency was the fact

that no patient was ever there long enough to get on your nerves. Not that you didn't form relationships in the relatively short time you looked after them. Emergency was a strange place. Here people were at their worst, the patients incredibly sick or scared, overwhelmed by the events that had bought them to this strange, fast-moving place. Emergency was such a contrast to the organised structure of the wards. Even the intimidating atmosphere of Intensive Care held a certain aura of calmness and quiet control.

Patients seemed to forget the staff in Emergency. The wards weren't lined with thank-you cards and the nurses' station didn't groan with the weight of flowers and chocolates from grateful patients.

Lila stood a moment after buzzing, waiting for permission to enter, her sleep-deprived brain forming an answer to the conundrum she had just raised. Maybe it was too painful for the patients and relatives to remember their time in Emergency. Maybe it was just a bit too close to the bone.

There was one thing Lila was sure of, though. The nurses in emergency never forgot the patients. Not tiny ones like this anyway.

As she looked at the blonde locks plastered to the tiny flushed face Lila swallowed a lump in her throat.

'How's she doing?'

'Good.' The optimism in the intensive care nurse's voice came as a delightful surprise. 'They're going to extubate her this morning. Touch wood, this one will be a happy ending.'

'And Amy, the little girl with meningococcal?'

'That miracle might take a bit longer.' The look that passed between the two women needed no words. With a small nod of thanks Lila made her way over to the glass window of the isolation ward and stood silently watching the little child swamped by machines and tubes, battling to stay with the world.

It wasn't fair. The mania of earlier had completely left her now and suddenly Lila felt incredibly deflated. Here was modern medicine at its best and still there were no answers, no guarantees.

'Shouldn't you be in bed?'

Declan's voice was half-expected. She had heard footsteps behind her and even before he'd spoken, the familiar tang of his aftershave, the gentleness of his presence had heralded his arrival.

'Not much point when you're lying there, wondering how they're doing. Sometimes it's easier to come and see for yourself.'

'I know.'

They both stood for a moment watching little Amy, watching and praying and hoping that it might, just might help.

'Are you off home?'

He shook his head. 'I'm stuck here, but just for

another hour or so and then I'm back again tonight. How about you?'

Lila shook her head. 'I've got a few nights off now.' A yawn escaped and she quickly covered her mouth. 'I'd best be off. Night, Declan, or should I say morning?'

'Night will do.'

Standing there, saying goodnight, was the hardest part of the whole night. The casualties, the emergencies she had been trained for. But nothing could have prepared her for this. Lila knew he was tired, exhausted even. And at another time, another place they would have been leaning on each other. Climbing into bed as the world worked on. Shutting the curtains on the world to create their own false night, slipping into sheets together, caressing each other's tired aching muscles, soothing each other with reassurances, erasing the scenes they had both witnessed.

Not standing in the bland corridor trying to freeze-frame his image, pretending the man she loved was just another colleague.

'Night, then.'

You could have had him. The words mocked her, taunted her, jeered her as she made her way home.

You could have had him.

CHAPTER NINE

RUNNING Elizabeth's bath, Lila perched on the edge and rested her tired face against the smooth cool tiles as she watched the bubbles multiply. Right up to a few days ago she could have had Declan. Even that vague dream had made the days more bearable, made the last eight years survivable. Surviving on the dream that maybe somehow, some day they might make it up again.

Except now he didn't want her. Declan was finally over her.

The tragic irony of it all was that only now, after eight long hard years, was she finally ready to accept the help she so desperately needed. Oh, she had never intended to throw her mother in a home and walk away, and it wasn't her intention now. But at last Lila had acknowledged that maybe the time had come to let go a little, to talk to Yvonne about a placement for Elizabeth, to loosen the reins and live a little herself.

Declan might never have left her emotionally but his physical return had forced Lila to re-examine her life, even as far as to mentally explore the possibility of a life with Declan, to free herself enough to accept the love he offered.

Had offered.

It was a cruel correction. She had left it too late, pushed him just too far and too many times, and now she had no one except herself to blame for the sheer loneliness she felt.

'You look exhausted.' Shirley flung open the door, wheeling Elizabeth in. 'Your mum's eaten all her breakfast so let's give her a bath and then you, my girl, can head off to bed.'

Lila smiled appreciatively at the prospect as she bent down and removed her mother's slippers. 'Sounds good to me.'

They worked well together, undressing Elizabeth and lowering her gently into the warm, soapy water as they chatted away.

Elizabeth had always seemed to enjoy her bath. Her contracted muscles relaxing slightly, her eyes closing as the water took her weight and the aroma of the oils Lila lovingly lavished into the water— they seemed to soothe her.

'Have you heard about the job yet?'

Lila shook her head as she shampooed her mother's hair. 'Not yet and I won't for a while, I expect. My boss had an accident last night so, no doubt, she'll be away for a few days.'

'It was just on the news about that house fire you

were telling me about.' Shirley tutted and shook her head. 'Poor little mites. But you said that you think they'll all be all right?'

'I think so. The intensive care staff seemed fairly optimistic.' Rinsing the last of the shampoo out of Elizabeth's hair, Lila managed a tired smile. 'Mind you, it did look pretty bleak there for a while. It's always so much harder when you're dealing with children.' She deliberately didn't depress Shirley with the details about Amy. Why ruin a happy ending? 'Pass me the conditioner, would you, Shirley?'

As Shirley leant over to get the bottle she paused. 'It just seems so unfair when it's a child. At least when someone older dies you know they've had a chance, a decent crack at life.' She smiled fondly at her sister as she squeezed a generous amount of conditioner onto Elizabeth's hair. 'Like your mother. I'm not saying it's not tragic what's happened, but she did have a good life—fifty-five wonderful years of sheer living before this horrible disease got to her.' When she looked up at her, Lila saw an urgency in her aunt's eyes that she hadn't seen before. 'And that's what you should be doing, darling, enjoying your life, living it. Who knows what's around the corner?'

Shirley wasn't one for introspection. She just drifted through life with a quiet air of optimism, a vague eccentricity that Lila adored. It was the closest she had ever come to giving Lila a lecture.

Pulling the plug, Lila felt her eyes fill up. Shirley was right, Declan was right, they all were.

Whether it was tiredness, emotion or perhaps a too generous splash of oil, as they lifted Elizabeth gently up Lila lost her grip. Over and over that split second she would go, reliving the instant she felt her mother slip, the desperate lurch to right herself and break Elizabeth's fall, Shirley's scream as Elizabeth fell from her arms, the sickening crunch as her mother landed on the floor.

Only Elizabeth stayed silent, her eyes open and staring. No yelp of pain or fear, just the never-ending silence of the world in which she lived.

Lila stood paralysed, her heart racing rapidly, the colour draining from her face. But as Shirley bent down to lift her, Lila's professionalism, ingrained into her, took over.

'Don't move her!'

Snapping into action, she bent over, carefully examining her mother for any sign of injury. One look at her short, rotated left leg and Lila knew her mother had broken her hip.

'Oh, Mum, I'm sorry.'

Shirley patted Lila on the shoulder, her voice trembling as she attempted to reassure her niece. 'It was an accident, pet. She's all right, it's not as if she was knocked out or anything. We should get her onto the bed. Maybe we should give her a sip of brandy or something, though. She's gone ever so pale.'

Lila shook her head, wiping her tears with the back of her hand. 'She's broken her hip, Shirley. I'll stay with her, you grab a duvet from the bed and call an ambulance.'

Lila knew the paramedics who arrived well. Well enough to know that the gentle handling of her mother, the quiet dignity they afforded her, weren't an act for her benefit. They were truly wonderful men. It made the wretched events seem somehow more bearable as they chatted amicably while they placed an oxygen mask over Elizabeth's face and started an intravenous infusion. They didn't just look after Elizabeth either—they reassured a shocked and trembling Lila every step of the way.

'I'll follow in the car with Ted,' Shirley suggested as the paramedics settled Elizabeth into the ambulance. 'You stay with your mum.'

The hospital was only twenty minutes away but it seemed to take for ever. Lila spent the journey telling Elizabeth over and over how much she loved her, how sorry she was for what had taken place.

It was only as the ambulance pulled up at her workplace that Lila felt a flutter of panic for herself. It was all going to be out in the open now—her lateness, her refusal to attend work functions, the reason she couldn't stay back after her shift without a phone call.

Everyone was going to know.

The difference now was that at last she was finally ready. Ready to accept the help that would inevitably be offered, ready for the inevitable changes that were about to occur.

'We're going to be fine, Mum,' Lila whispered. 'We're going to be fine, just you wait and see.'

Taking a deep, calming breath, she held Elizabeth's hand as the ambulance doors opened.

'Declan!' The concerned face that met her as the ambulance door was opened was the last one she'd expected, but the most welcoming sight she had ever seen. 'I thought you'd be at home.'

They stood aside as the paramedics unloaded Elizabeth and wheeled her into the department.

'I nearly was.' His usual smiling face was creased with concern. 'I was just about to leave when Ambulance Control alerted us you were on your way. I wanted to see for myself how you were both doing.'

In all the drama it had never even entered her head that Ambulance Control would alert the hospital even though they had done the same thing for Hester just last night. Lila was infinitely grateful for the foresight.

Infinitely grateful that Declan was there.

'I lost my grip when we were lifting her out of the

bath.' A sob escaped her lips and she broke down. 'She's broken her hip...'

'We don't know that yet, Lila...'

'Oh, come on, Declan, I know I'm not the best nurse in the world but give me some credit. She's broken her hip, I'm telling you! I dropped her, Declan, I dropped my own mother.'

He held her then. Right there in the middle of the ambulance bay. Oblivious of the cars and personnel going about their business. He just held her close and let her cry, sharing her pain, her exhaustion, her utter grief.

And finally, when the tears were slowing and the gulping, shuddering breaths had abated slightly, he pulled back. His fingers tilted her chin to make her look at him.

'It was an accident, Lila, an accident.'

And as she gazed back at him, she saw the years they had lost together with painful, aching clarity. Saw the wisdom he had gained, the strength that came with maturity, the tiny lines a permanent reminder of his frequent smile.

Never had she wanted to lean on him more.

'Let's go and see how she's doing, huh?' And taking her hand, he led her slowly inside.

The department was full, a combination of the events of the previous night and a busy morning. The curious, sympathetic looks from her colleagues didn't embarrass Lila, though. Amazingly, they actually helped.

Moira, the charge nurse, bustled in. 'Can you not stay away from the place for five minutes, Lila?' She joked, her thick Irish accent lilting and soft. 'I'll just find another pair of hands and we can get your ma into a gown and some obs done. I'll get Mr Hinkley round to see her straight away.'

'There's no need,' Lila said quickly.

'Mr Hinkley will want to see your mother, to be sure,' Moira insisted. 'You're staff, Lila.'

'I know the protocol but honestly, Moira, you're not dealing with Hester, saying no when she means yes. I'd really rather Declan looked after her.'

There was firmness in Lila's voice that left no room for doubt and with a small shrug Moira gave Declan a saucy wink. 'And when did you earn your stripes, young man? Right, let's get this gown on.'

'I'll do it,' Lila offered.

'You will not,' Declan led her gently to a chair. 'You look terrible, as if you're about to pass out or something. *I'll* help Moira and then we'll get her straight around to X-Ray.'

She was too tired to argue. Sitting down, she suddenly felt acutely aware of the scruffy, faded shorts she had pulled on after her own shower, her wet hair trailing down her back, her face for once void of even a trace of make-up.

No wonder he thought she looked awful.

His back was to her, and she watched as he carefully pulled a gown over Elizabeth's emaciated arms, gently lifting her forward a fraction to tuck the gown in behind her. She took in the wide shoulders, the tidy trim of his hair, the muscular legs in well-fitting trousers.

What she didn't see was the look that passed between Declan and Moira as they looked at the lovingly painted finger- and toenails on Elizabeth, the obvious love and devotion that had gone into keeping the emaciated woman's skin so intact. She didn't see the glaze of tears in his eyes as he wrapped the blood-pressure cuff around his patient's arm, the flicker of his Adam's apple as he swallowed back the lump in his throat.

'Her obs are all pretty good, Lila, and she doesn't seem distressed, but you're right—her hip is obviously broken.' She was too wrapped up in her own guilt to hear the tremble in his voice. Turning, he flashed her his 'doctor' smile. 'I think that we ought to give her an injection of pethidine in case she is in any pain, then I'll organise to get her straight around for an X-ray.'

The curtains were pulled open and Shirley rushed in, with Ted following anxiously behind. 'Sorry we took so long, darling. The ambulance just whizzed off and then it took ages to find a parking space.' She hugged her niece. 'What did the doctor say?'

Lila hugged her aunt back. 'She's just going for an X-ray but Declan's pretty sure that she's broken her hip.'

'Declan!' Shirley looked over sharply. 'Declan Haversham! I don't believe it. My goodness, it is you!' Her face broke into a huge grin. 'I haven't seen you in years. How are you? I can't get over this.' She looked from Declan to Lila. 'Imagine him being on this morning. It's fate, that's what it is. It must be a shock for you too, Lila, seeing him again after all these years.'

'I've been here quite a few weeks now,' Declan said lightly, in stark contrast to Shirley's excited tones. 'I expect the shock's worn off a bit by now.'

'But you never even mentioned he was back, Lila,' Shirley admonished, oblivious to the tension that suddenly filled the cubicle, adding with painful clarity. 'Why didn't you say anything?'

It was Declan who saved her from answering. 'I expect Lila didn't think it was very important.' There was an edge to his voice that even Shirley heeded and the sudden strained atmosphere was only broken when the porter appeared to take Elizabeth for her X-ray.

* * *

Even before Declan clipped the films onto the viewing box Lila knew what the results of the X-rays would be.

'I'll get the orthopods down straight away.'

'Do you think they'll operate today?' Lila's voice was a little wobbly.

'It's fairly unstable and she'll be bleeding quite a lot but I doubt they'll rush her up. They'll probably spend today giving her a medical work-up, perhaps a blood transfusion. Get her as stable as possible before they operate.'

Declan was spot on as usual. Marcus Hastings, the orthopaedic consultant, almost echoed Declan's words as he relayed his findings to the anxious family.

'I think the operation should be performed today, but I'd like her to have a medical work-up before I take her to Theatre. I'm going to be operating through till about nine tonight and I think I'll add your mother to the end of the list. Once she's had a couple of units of blood and a few hours of oxygen and fluids she'll be a much better candidate for Theatre. Obviously the anaesthetist will have to asses her but I'd also like to ask Yvonne Selles, the geriatrician, to have a look at her, possibly with a view to admitting her under shared care between the geriatricians and orthopods.'

Lila held her breath. This was the first push that would start the ball rolling in the inevitable direction of a nursing home. Once the allied health services assessed Elizabeth, the result would be a foregone conclusion. But she couldn't think about that right now. The important thing was to get her mother's hip fracture stabilised.

'Why don't you go home, Lila?' Shirley's suggestion was as unexpected as it was ludicrous.

'Of course I'm not going to go home. I'm not going to just leave her!'

'You won't just be leaving your mum. I'll be with her. What can you do here?' Shirley reasoned. 'You've been working all night, and no doubt you're going to want to be here when they operate. Why don't you take a taxi home and have a little rest? Then you can come back this evening when they're getting your mum ready for Theatre. If you stay here all day and night, you're going to make yourself ill.'

'She's right.' Declan wasted no time agreeing with Shirley.

'But it's a twenty-minute drive from home,' Lila protested. 'What if something happened? I might not get back in time.'

'Lila, you need some sleep.' Declan's tone was firm. 'Look, I'm going home myself now. Why don't you crash at my place instead of taking a taxi home? I'm literally two minutes away from the hospital, so if there's any change in your mum's condition you can get back here quickly. I'm due back on duty at eight anyway. I can bring you in to see Elizabeth on my way to work, long before she's due to go to Theatre.'

'That's sorted, then,' Shirley enthused. 'It will give you two a chance to catch up. I'm sure you've got loads to talk about after all these years.'

'I'm not exactly in the mood for a trip down memory lane,' Lila said pointedly. The last thing she wanted was for Declan to feel she had any master plan behind all of this. He had extended the hand of friendship in the same way he would have for any colleague in this situation. And it was up to her to behave like one.

'If there's any change, you'll call,' Lila checked reluctantly.

'Of course. Now, you go and get some sleep.'

Sleep! With Declan in the next room and her mother waiting for an operation? Shirley had really lost the plot this time!

After kissing her mother tenderly, Lila waited as Declan scribbled down his home number.

'Come on, Nurse Bailey.' Declan threw a casual arm around her shoulder and gave her an affectionate squeeze. 'Let's get you to bed.'

She was still too upset and reeling from the morning's events to be embarrassed at being back at Declan's.

Well, almost.

'Have you had breakfast?' he asked, pulling open the fridge as she stood there somewhat lost in the middle of the kitchen.

'I'm not hungry.'

'Good. There's not exactly a lot of choice.' He held up half a black avocado and a lettuce that had seen better days. 'Unfortunately Yvonne's a worse shopper than me. There's eggs!' he added with a triumphant note.

Lila made her way over and, standing beside him, peered into the bare fridge. Yvonne's timely entrance into the conversation hadn't gone unnoticed and she struggled to keep her voice light. 'Eggs that expired a week ago. You haven't changed that much! Look, why don't you go and grab a shower? I'll see what I can rustle up.'

Declan grinned. 'So you can accuse me of being chauvinist? You're *my* guest, Lila, I should be cooking for you.'

'I'd hardly call buttering some toast cooking. Go on.'

Hearing the water from his shower running a few minutes later, Lila put the kettle on. She still couldn't quite believe she was here, that the image she had dared to dream about this morning as she'd been in ICU was actually happening.

'Dream on,' she muttered, salvaging some rather stale-looking bread from the cupboard.

But she couldn't help it if her mind wandered when Declan appeared again, his shoulders still wet from the shower, a pair of boxer shorts the only piece of clothing covering his gorgeous body. His hair was black and curly and she could smell the soap and deodorant and the tang of aftershave. He seemed fresh, exuberant, not someone who'd been awake for the last twenty-four hours.

His appetite hadn't diminished over the years either and the toaster was kept busy for a while as he ravished the best part of the loaf. Lila nibbled on hers just for the sake of it. The vision of her mother falling to the floor still too recent for her to have any appetite.

'How are you doing?' he asked finally when it was obvious Lila wasn't going to be making any small talk.

'Not the best. I think I should maybe head back to the hospital. I'm never going to sleep.'

'Even if you just stretch out for a while and relax, it will do you some good. I was on with you last night, remember, Lila. I know how exhausted you must be.'

When she didn't answer he lowered himself from the bar stool and came over. 'Lila, don't beat yourself up, it wasn't your fault.'

'Of course it was my fault,' she snapped. 'I was the one who dropped her, Declan. If Mum dies from this—'

'Stop right there.' His voice was firm but Lila ignored him.

'Why? Are you going to try and tell me that there's no chance of that happening? That she's not going to die?'

'You know I can't do that. But, Lila, what I can tell you is that your mother is frail and her bones are fragile and what happened this morning was a simple accident—with tragic consequences, yes, but an accident all the same. You have nothing to feel guilty about, you've done everything humanly possible for your mother.'

But she steadfastly refused to be comforted. The one time she had let her mind wander, allowed herself a glimpse of a life without nursing her mother, this had happened.

'Come on, you.' Helping her off the bar stool, Declan led her up the stairs and into his bedroom. Gently laying her on the bed, he pulled the curtains on the hot midday sun.

Pickling up the alarm clock from the bedside, he gave her a lazy smile. 'I'll come and wake you around seven. You try and rest, you look completely done in.'

'Where will you sleep?' Lila flushed, glad of the

darkened room. She hadn't been fishing yet still she held her breath as she awaited his answer. But Declan wasn't giving anything away.

'Don't worry about me, Lila. You try and get some rest.'

His hand running down her cheek felt so intrinsically right, almost an extension of herself, that it took a moment to register it was even there.

'You poor thing,' he said softly.

His sudden tenderness, the empathy in his words struck at the very core of her. Catching his hand, she held it to her cheek for a moment as if somehow his strength might seep into her.

'Declan?'

He didn't answer, just stood there and stared down at her, his face unreadable in the dark shadows.

'I know that we're just friends, I know it's over between us, but…' She swallowed nervously, unsure of what she was saying, her words utterly unrehearsed, her feelings at this moment unprecedented. All she knew for sure was being alone right now was the last thing she wanted.

And Declan, however unattainable, however out of her life, was the one person who might be able to give her the peace she craved. 'Can you lie here with me, just for old times' sake? I don't want to be alone right now.'

He didn't say anything for an age, just stood there

in the darkness, his breathing heavy, his hand still resting on her cheek.

'Sure.'

She felt the mattress move as he lay beside her, felt the warmth that radiated from him. They lay rigidly apart, Declan's hands tucked behind his head as he gazed at the ceiling.

It had been a stupid idea, Lila realised all too quickly. She had been a fool to suggest it. Declan obviously didn't want to be here and she had forced him into it. He felt as awkward as hell, and so did she.

But just as Lila thought she would die with shame she felt the tension suddenly seep out of him.

'Come here.' His voice was thick, soft and she felt his arm reach out to her, pulling her into his embrace.

With her head on his chest and his arm tightly around her, she lay there, breathing him in, his free hand stroking her thick blonde hair.

And slowly her awkwardness diminished, the horror of the day receded and in Declan's arms she drifted into the sweetest, deepest sleep.

Only when dusk crept in, when the hum of the rush-hour traffic died down and the shadows around the curtains were replaced by darkness did she wake up.

Stirring gently, the drama of what had happened filtered in, overwhelming her in an instant. But nothing, not even her mother's fall, prepared her for the loss she felt when she reached out and felt an empty space. Declan's side of the bed was cold and the alarm clock was gone.

Hearing the whirring of the automatic garage door opening, Lila lay there, frozen. Yvonne was home.

Was that the reason for his defection? Declan didn't want to answer to his new girlfriend!

Her ears on elastic, she lay there in the darkness, listening to the key turn in the door, willing Declan to speak, but the silence of the house only grew louder. She heard Yvonne's footsteps on the stairs, the echo of her heels on the floorboards, the creaking of the next door as Yvonne entered her bedroom. Pulling the duvet over her head in an effort to block out the image that had suddenly invaded her mind, Lila lay there praying for a reprieve, praying she'd somehow read it all wrong.

But when she heard their muffled voices, heard Declan stretch and yawn, it was as if a knife had been plunged straight into her heart.

'Poor Lila,' he had said. Poor Lila all right, poor desperate Lila, desperate for any crumbs of comfort he offered. Living in the past, unable to move on.

It took every ounce of effort she possessed not to go get dressed and run out of the house there and then, and even more to smile brightly when Declan walked into the bedroom an hour later and placed a steaming mug on the bedside table beside her.

Rubbing feigned sleep from her eyes, Lila yawned widely.

'How long have you been up?' she asked innocently.

'Only just.'

Taking a sip, she lifted her eyes to his face. 'Really? I didn't hear you move.'

'You were sound asleep,' he lied so easily. 'I thought I'd let you sleep for a bit longer.'

Her only consolation was that his eyes didn't quite meet hers.

CHAPTER TEN

'SIT down, Lila, for heaven's sake. You're making me nervous.' Shirley patted the chair beside her. 'The theatre nurse said it would be at least another hour before we heard anything.'

'Do you want a coffee?' Lila swung round, completely oblivious to the words her aunt had just spoken.

'No, Lila,' Shirley replied patiently. 'I want you to sit down. Come on, darling, tell me about Declan. I can't believe you didn't tell me he was back on the scene.'

'He isn't,' Lila said grimly. 'We just happen to work together.'

'So what was it like, seeing him again after all these years?'

The incessant pacing starting again. 'This is hardly the place for a cosy girls' talk.'

Shirley, completely unperturbed by her niece's sharp words, rummaged in her bag and produced a bar of chocolate. 'I'd say it's exactly the place. What's wrong with a touch of reminiscing to take your mind of what's going on in there?' Shirley gestured to the bland beige swing doors with STAFF

ONLY BEYOND THIS POINT emblazoned across them. 'Your mum would have loved to catch up with Declan again, she thought the world of him. It seems fitting somehow that he's the doctor treating her.'

Lila had had her doubts in the past about the planet that Shirley inhabited, but now her suspicions were confirmed—Shirley really did dance to a different drum!

Swinging round, she gave her aunt an incredulous look. 'She hated Declan, didn't trust him as far as she could throw him—and those were Mum's words, not mine.'

Shirley broke the bar and handed Lila half. 'Rubbish, that was just her illness talking. Most of the time she adored him.'

With painstaking slowness she peeled the silver foil back from her half of the chocolate. Carefully breaking a piece off, she popped it into her mouth. Only when Shirley finally looked up did she register the look of utter confusion on Lila's face.

'Your mother adored him,' she said. 'Remember our wedding anniversary, that turkey dance Declan did…?'

'Chicken dance, but—'

'That's the one, and then the hokey-cokey. I've never seen your mum laugh so much.'

'She said he was a no-good student, good for nothing…' Lila argued.

'But he stood up to her. ''Ah, but one day this good-for-nothing student will be a doctor, Elizabeth, and won't you be proud of your daughter then, married to…''' her voice trailed off as she saw the tears streaming down Lila's cheeks.

'It was her illness, pet, that made her say those things. She didn't even trust my Ted, said he was just like your dad. My Ted, for heaven's sake. He's the most decent man I've ever met and I'm not saying that just because he's my husband. She even accused the vicar of pilfering the collection tray at one point.' Shirley put out her hand, pulling Lila to the seat beside her. 'Oh, sweetie, she loved him, we all did. We were devastated when you broke up. I know we all said you were better of without him and all that, but that was just what family say—that was just us sticking up for you.'

No respecter of a crisis, Shirley popped the last of the chocolate into her mouth then nearly choked as the realisation dawned.

'You didn't finish with him because of what your mum said?'

'No,' Lila answered defiantly, but her voice broke as the word tumbled out. 'Well, partly. He laughed at me, Shirley, he laughed when I said I was going to do nursing. He should have been—'

'We all laughed, Lila,' Shirley said gently. 'We all laughed at the thought. Heavens above, you fainted at a gory movie. None of us ever thought for a moment you'd do it.'

'But I did.'

'Yes, pet, you did, you proved us all wrong. Is there any chance of you two making it up after all this time?'

Lila sniffed, accepting the handkerchief her aunt offered.

'I thought there might be when he first came back, but I messed everything up—again,' she added, blowing her nose loudly. 'I thought he was living with another woman. It turned out he wasn't, they were just house-sharing, and anyway it just seemed so impossible, with Mum being sick and everything.'

'But nothing's impossible. If you love each other you can work anything out.'

'A nice theory.' Lila shook her head. 'I treated him terribly, and now he's decided to move on once and for all. I can't say I blame him. He told me he was going to ask Yvonne, that's the woman I was worried about, out for a drink.'

'A drink?' Shirley scoffed. 'That's hardly a marriage proposal. You can deal with that!'

'That was a while ago,' Lila said sadly. 'It would seem things have moved pretty quickly since then. They're sleeping together.'

Her aunt's arms wrapped around Lila's heaving shoulders. 'What a mess, what a sorry mess.'

Lila managed a wry grin through her tears. 'I think at this point you're supposed to be saying it was all for the best, that I'm better of without him anyway.'

Shirley didn't answer for a while. The ticking of the clock seemed to suddenly grow louder and when finally Shirley did speak, her voice was heavy, full of weary insight. 'But you're not, Lila, are you? You're not better off without him.'

The operation went well, at least that's what the surgeon said, but seeing her mother so pale and fragile back on the ward Lila had never felt more scared or alone.

'How's she doing?'

Declan's voice was a hoarse whisper so as not to wake the other patients. She felt his hot, dry hand over hers on the starched linen sheets and immediately withdrew hers.

'Apparently it went well.' She hadn't intended to move her hand so pointedly but the conversation with Shirley was still ringing in her ears and Lila felt as if her soul were exposed to the world. That any touch, however fleeting, however well meaning, might somehow transfer the true depth of her feelings.

He stood there awkwardly. Her blatant rebuff hadn't gone unnoticed.

'Yvonne's going to take over her care now, that's

why they've admitted her to the acute geriatric unit. Of course, the orthos will review their handiwork but the geriatric team is going to oversee her recovery. From what the charge nurse said, they can arrange all sorts of allied health services for me from the ward.'

'That's good.' His words were kind, with no trace of patronage.

'We'll see.' With a sigh she slipped off the bed and wandered out into the ward corridor. 'I've been doing a lot of thinking. I'm starting to think that a home might be better for her.'

'It was an accident, Lila.'

'I know,' she finally admitted. 'I was actually coming around to the idea beforehand. It's not that I don't want to look after her, it's just I don't think I can physically do it any more.'

'But maybe with the right help it would be easier. Look, Lila, you've had it so tough up until now. Surely now everything's out in the open, things can only improve. If nursing your mum at home is what you really want to do, go for it.'

His words were a revelation, the antithesis of what she'd expected to hear. 'I didn't think you'd understand. I thought that you'd just agree she's better off in a home.'

'It's not about what I think, Lila, or any of us for that matter. It's about what you want. It's about supporting your decisions and doing our best to make it as easy on you as possible. Lila, I don't want to upset you further but I think we both know that your mum hasn't got much longer. You've come this far. If you want to see it through to the end, don't lose your confidence now.'

He put his arm around her as she started to weep. 'This is about you, Lila...'

The sudden shrill of his pager made them both jump. Looking down at the small black pager pinned to his white coat, he frowned. 'They need me back.'

I need you, Lila wanted to scream, but of course she didn't. 'Thanks for coming by.' How austere her words sounded, such a contrast to the violent emotions engulfing her as she stood there.

Stood there and watched Declan leave.

Even though orthopaedics wasn't her specialty, as a nurse Lila knew more or less the care her mother would receive. Or at least she'd thought she did. But though it initially felt strange, watching others deliver the care she was so used to giving, what came as a bigger and more pleasant surprise was the way in which that care was delivered. The empathy shown by the nurses, the diligent attention to detail, the kind, gentle words that soothed Elizabeth as they turned and washed her.

What Lila had expected she wasn't sure. Always

fiercely proud of her profession, for some reason when it came to her own mother to this day she had been sure only she, Lila, could truly provide what Elizabeth needed. But now...

'Doctor Selles will see you now.'

'Thank you.' Putting Elizabeth's hairbrush back into the locker, Lila followed the charge nurse to Yvonne's office. At this morning's ward round Lila had asked Yvonne if she might have a word to discuss her mother's care after her discharge. It was a huge step and one Lila was still undecided about, but at least now she was prepared to listen to the options.

'Lila, have a seat.'

Yvonne looked rather uncomfortable, which came as no surprise. They weren't exactly on the best of terms and having to deal with Lila in a professional capacity couldn't have been easy for Yvonne.

'I'm pleased you've asked to discuss your mother's post-hospital care. Declan did bring your mother's issues to my attention even before Elizabeth's accident.' She watched Lila's reaction.

'Good. He said he was going to.'

'Now, I understand you're opposed to your mother going into a nursing home—can I ask why? I mean, I know it's never an easy decision, but what are your specific concerns?'

Lila took a deep breath. She liked the directness of Yvonne's questions, and had no hesitation in answering her honestly. After all, it was her mother's future that was being discussed.

'I'm worried that she won't get the right attention in a home. Working in Emergency, unfortunately I've seen first hand the byproducts of the less than satisfactory nursing care some of the homes deliver.'

'But there are good homes,' Yvonne said gently. 'One of the negatives of our job is that you only get to see things when they go wrong. On the other side of the coin there are numerous elderly people in nursing homes, receiving the best of care and attention.'

'I know,' Lila admitted. 'And I've also been very pleasantly surprised at the care Mum's got in here, it's given me a lot of confidence. So much so that I'm considering looking at a few homes—nothing definite, mind,' she added quickly. 'But in the meantime, while I decide, I would like to see about getting some help for me at home with Mum. The accident really frightened me, and I realise now that I do need help, for Mum's sake if nothing else.'

Yvonne gave her a sympathetic smile. 'I'll arrange the allied health worker to come and speak with you and run through some of the options that are available to you, though I don't envisage your mother being discharged for some time yet. As I told you this morning, it's a big operation for someone so frail and it will be a while before we even think about sending her home.'

Lila stood up. 'Thanks for your time, Yvonne.'

'No problem, I'm happy to help. Oh, and, Lila…'

Lila watched as the beginnings of a blush crept across Yvonne's cheeks.

'About all that business at the emergency ball. I just thought I'd better explain—'

Lila waved her hand dismissively. 'Please, Yvonne, there's really no need.'

'But there is, Lila, there's every need. I want to be sure that you don't have any concerns—I mean, with the fact that it's me looking after your mother. I want you to be assured that your mother is getting the very best care available.'

'I know that she is, Yvonne, and I'm grateful to all the staff here for that, you included.'

'Thank you. Look, Lila, I'm sorry if this sounds inappropriate but, given the circumstances, I think some honesty is called for. I just want to be sure that everything is really over between you and Declan. It's just…well, we're going out for dinner tonight and he's warned me that there's something big that he wants to ask me. I just don't want to rock the boat. Things are difficult enough as it is.'

Suddenly Yvonne's accent didn't sound so lyrical any more; 'grating' would have been a more apt word.

Lila stood up smartly. 'You're right, Yvonne.' She was too tired to bother being polite. 'That probably was a bit inappropriate, but don't worry. I'm not going to collapse in a heap when I hear the happy news. You never know, I might even throw a note in the collection envelope.' And turning smartly on her heel, she left the stuffy confines of Yvonne's office.

'Lila, it's so good to see you. I was actually just about to pop, or should I say hobble, up to the ward and pay you both a visit—you've saved me a trip. How is your mother doing?' Hester's rather endearing welcome took Lila back somewhat, and she smothered a smile as Moira pulled a comical face behind Hester's shoulder.

'Well, the operation went well, but it's still very early days. I was actually hoping to go through my off-duty shifts with you. I'm on days off at the moment and I thought I'd better confirm that I *will* be back at work tomorrow night, but once Mum's discharged I might need to take a few days' annual leave.'

Hester picked up the roster. 'Well, let's have a look, shall we? We may as well grab a coffee and take it to my office. It will be nice to have a chat.' And hobbling off on her fibreglass plaster, she left a bemused and grinning Lila staring in disbelief at her departing rear.

'What painkillers did they prescribe her?'

Moira tutted loudly. 'Only the good Lord above

knows what's going on in that woman's mind. She's arranging a staff barbecue next weekend and she's even filled the biscuit barrel for the first time this century. I reckon that knock on her head must have been more serious than Declan realised.'

'Oh, well.' Lila laughed. 'Better not spoil the good mood by keeping her waiting. And, Moira, thanks for all your help with Mum the other day.'

Moira patted Lila's arm affectionately. 'Not at all. We're all glad to help, don't even mention it.'

Hester even made the coffee. Opening the roster, she stared at it for a moment.

'It might be a bit of a struggle,' she started, and Lila closed her eyes.

Here we go again, she thought, anything to make my life a bit more difficult.

'It's always harder replacing an associate charge nurse than an RN.' She smiled as Lila opened her eyes abruptly.

'You mean...'

'That's right, the position's yours! Congratulations—that is, assuming you still want the job?'

Lila nodded enthusiastically. 'Oh, yes, I want it. I just wasn't expecting it.'

'It's well deserved. I'm not going to pretend I didn't initially have my reservations about giving it to you, but let's just say they were all dispelled the other night. You did an excellent job under extremely trying circumstances. A lot of more experienced staff would have panicked and started calling staff in. You handled it all very well, utilising the staff available as well as calling in a few favours.' She paused, seeing Lila's frown. 'Gerard Harper, the paediatric consultant, wouldn't call colleagues in on a nurse's say-so unless he respected you greatly. Even the surgical resident acted as a teaboy, and it's all credit to you. Your methods have been a wake-up call, even for a cynic like me.

'Now, I'm not saying I'm suddenly going to be everyone's best friend but I can see your point more clearly.'

Lila was blushing to her roots, completely floored by her boss's flattering comments, but Hester hadn't finished with her yet.

'Nurse Bailey, am I really that unapproachable?' When Lila didn't immediately respond she continued. 'Why couldn't you come to me and tell me about your mother? Surely it could have helped? At least if I'd known then I would have understood the pressure you were under, the reason for your lateness…'

Lila shook her head. 'It wasn't just you, Hester, I didn't tell anyone how things were at home.'

'But why? You're the one who insists on a friendly atmosphere, comradeship, supporting one's colleagues.'

'I know,' Lila admitted. 'It just all seemed too big at the time. I realise now it would have been easier all round just to open up a bit.'

Hester nodded thoughtfully. 'Well, now that we do all know, will you at least come to me if there is a problem?' She smiled as Lila nodded. 'And as to the roster, just let me know when the time comes that you need a few days. If we can't arrange cover perhaps I could do a stint of nights myself. Don't look so shocked! I don't turn into a pumpkin at midnight.'

Lila made her way back to her mother's side in time to feed Elizabeth her evening meal, but despite all her encouragement and cajoling she didn't manage to get more than a couple of teaspoons into her.

'Would you like me to have a go?'

Lila smiled at the young nurse. 'Please, Lorna. I've given up on the main course but she won't even take the custard and she normally enjoys that.'

But even with Lorna's best attempts, Elizabeth simply wasn't interested.

'We might give her a break for now and try her with a fortified drink a bit later,' Lorna suggested. 'Let her have a little rest and I'll come back to her later before I go off. Do you want to give me a hand with her pressure-area care?'

'Sure.' The nurses had been marvellous. Aware that Lila was Elizabeth's primary care-giver, they had included her wherever possible in her mother's care, never once assuming they knew best.

Once she was changed and settled, Lila gave her mother a fond kiss. 'I might head off home, catch up on some sleep,' Lila told Lorna. 'I'm supposed to be starting back at work tomorrow night.'

'You know you can pop up any time, even on your break, and sit with her a while.'

Lila nodded. 'I know. You've all been great.' Her hand lingered on her mother's forehead. 'You will remember to try her with the feed tonight?'

'I promise.'

Lila flushed. 'Sorry, I'm interfering again.'

'Don't be daft, she's your mother.'

And though she meant to go, for some reason Lila dragged the chair over again. Holding Elizabeth's hand, she chatted a while longer, recalling days long since gone, reliving memories of happy times, good times, barely noticing when Lorna flicked the lights off and plunged the ward into semi-darkness.

Happy that Elizabeth was settled for a sleep, Lila groped on the floor for her bag, making sure her keys and mobile were all where they should be. Only after she had kissed her mother goodnight did she look up, just in time to see Yvonne coming out of her office, hurriedly locking the door behind her, a flushed, radiant smile filling her face which could only mean that the footsteps approaching belonged to Declan.

She watched from the shadows as Yvonne turned

to greet him, watched from the wings as they made their way out of the ward.

Watched as her life dissolved around her.

It was strange, not having her mother at home, not having the evening meal and bath to deal with, the nightly turns.

And for the first time in ages Lila didn't collapse exhausted in front of the television at nine o'clock.

'Fancy a glass of wine, Shirley?' she asked, pulling the cork on a bottle of red.

'You know, actually I do.'

Shirley hardly ever drank but after the week they'd shared a glass or two seemed more than merited.

'It's strange without your mum here, isn't it, darling? I mean, I know she didn't talk or anything but…'

'I was just thinking same thing.'

Tucking her feet under her on the sofa, Lila tried to chatter away with Shirley, and later tried to concentrate on the late night film. Anything other than think what Declan and Yvonne were doing right now.

But red wine and slushy films didn't mix, at least not when you were lugging about a broken heart.

It was a relief to go to bed and give way to her tears.

CHAPTER ELEVEN

'SOMEONE slept well.' Shirley placed a round of toast and a huge milky mug of coffee on the heavy wooden table. 'You must have a clear conscience.'

Lila yawned as she pulled out a chair and sat down. 'More's the pity. A dose of decadence would suit me fine right now.' Eyeing the bacon Shirley was lavishly loading onto her toast, Lila laughed. 'You're not very good for my figure. At this rate—'

The ringing of the telephone didn't stall their conversation. Tossing her hair as she grabbed the receiver, Lila made a casual comment about cellulite and answered the telephone with an innocence she was about to lose.

'What is it?' Shirley stood there, alerted by the anxious tones in her niece's voice, the pan raised dangerously in the air, the smell of bacon suddenly making Lila feel nauseous.

'Mum's developed a chest infection. They want us to come straight up to the hospital.'

Shirley gave a reassuring smile. 'There's a lot of them going around right now. They'll give her some antibiotics and she'll be fine. Ted was coughing like an old train...'

'Shirley.' There was something in Lila's voice that stopped Shirley in her tracks. 'This is serious.'

'How serious?'

Lila looked at the ceiling, biting her lip as two huge tears splashed onto her cheeks. Her voice was audible but there was a tremor as she spoke. 'I think this might be it.'

Strange, the things you thought about. As they piled into the car, she leant her face against the car window, watching the world carrying on as normal. The line of people at the tram stop, on their way to work. Mr Cole taking his dog for a walk. Schoolchildren chatting as they ambled along.

The charge nurse had been gentle with her words but the message had been brutal, and Lila was under no misconception that she was going to see her mother for the last time.

How many times had she rung relatives? Told them not to rush, it was pointless having an accident on the way, but to come now nonetheless.

Her instinct was to rush to her mother's bedside, but the charge nurse was waiting for them. 'Dr Selles would like to have a word first.'

Lila shook her head. Diagnoses, prognoses, they were all immaterial, the need to see her mother surpassed everything. 'I want to see my mum now.'

It was the first time she had dug her heels in where

her mother was concerned and after a brief pause the charge nurse nodded.

'I'll take you to her now.'

Elizabeth didn't look very different. Her cheeks were flushed, her face wet with perspiration, but apart from that she looked much the same as when Lila had left her last night. Her hair had been brushed and even the usual slick of lipstick was in place, a credit to Lorna who smiled at Lila though her eyes glistened with tears.

'Shall I take you to speak with the doctor now?'

A gentle hand guided her elbow, helping her the short distance to Yvonne's office where Ted and Shirley sat in strained silence.

'I was just explaining to your aunt that Elizabeth has developed serious pneumonia. We've taken a lot of bloods and X-rays, and unfortunately it's very grave.'

Ever the optimist, Shirley broke in quickly. 'But surely it can be treated. I know that when my Uncle Vince had—'

'Shirley.' Lila halted her aunt, her eyes turning to Yvonne as the doctor continued with her grim news.

'She needs to go on a ventilator,' Yvonne didn't blind them with science, didn't tell them the direness of Elizabeth's blood-gas results. It would have gone completely over Shirley's and Ted's heads and for Lila it was too much to take in. 'She also needs much stronger antibiotics. That would involve frequent blood tests to check the levels and the antibiotics themselves are not without risks, particularly as Elizabeth does have some renal impairment. But even if we do move her across to ICU and put her on a ventilator—'

'No.' It was Lila that interrupted Yvonne this time.

'No,' she repeated softly as every eye in the room turned to her. 'Enough is enough.'

They were the toughest words she had ever uttered, the hardest decision she had ever made, but she knew in her heart it was the right one. Her mother had suffered enough, and to prolong the agony would be cruel.

'Lila, if you want to get a second opinion I quite understand.'

For a second Lila stiffened. Staring at her hands, she blinked back tears. For that instant she hated Yvonne. It was an alien feeling, one that Lila had never had before. Yvonne, with her soft, lilting voice, her immaculate clothes, seemed to impinge on her life in the most abhorrent way. The two people she loved most in the world were lost to her and Yvonne, however unwittingly, had played a role in each of them. But as Lila looked up at the other woman, she saw her for what she was, not the best friend a girl could wish for but a caring, compassionate doctor nonetheless, who had done her best to save Elizabeth.

Unfortunately it was a war that couldn't be won—by anyone.

There was nothing to hate.

'That won't be necessary.'

Shirley blew her nose loudly. 'What now, Doctor?'

'You might want to sit with her, spend some time with her.'

Shirley stood up. 'Come on, pet, let's go and see your mum.'

But Lila shook her head. 'I need to get some air. You go, Shirley. Tell Mum I'll be along soon.'

The air wasn't particularly fresh outside Emergency, but she stood there with the smokers, watching the ambulances rush past, watching the hubbub of the hospital as she sipped on a cup of machine-made hot chocolate.

Somehow she needed this time alone, time to prepare herself for whatever lay ahead.

'Nurse Bailey?'

Lila swung around, trying desperately to put a name to the face that was smiling at her. 'Jessica?'

'That's right. I'm surprised you remember.'

'Of course I remember. Mind you, you're looking a lot better than the last time I saw you. I take it you're on your way home?'

Jessica nodded. 'Mark's bringing the car around. I was just heading into Casualty to leave these for you.' Handing a large bunch of flowers to Lila, Jessica blushed. 'I was going to ask if I could leave these for you for when you came back on duty.'

Lila was touched, deeply touched, and told her so.

'You helped me a lot that night. I know I was pretty out of it and everything, but, well, I remember how you took the time to listen and tell me to take the help that was offered...'

'And did you?'

Jessica nodded. 'I'm having counselling, and they've put me on some medication, and I'll get there. I know that now. Mark's been wonderful. I did what you said and tried talking to him. I should have done it months ago.'

As Mark pulled up in the car, Lila gave the woman a quick hug. 'Look after yourself, Jessica.'

So the patients did remember after all. Burying her face in the heady fragrance of the bouquet, Lila tried to summon the strength to head back upstairs.

'More flowers from your admirers?'

'If I told you this was only the second bunch I've received in eight years, would you believe me?'

Declan laughed. 'Probably not.'

He looked fresh and bright, not a trace of the night's excesses marring his complexion. 'I've just been up to ICU to check on little Amy, and guess what? She's been moved to the kids' ward.'

She tried to smile. It was great news after all, but right now it was more than she could muster.

'I need to talk to you, Lila.' There was an anxious edge to his voice

'Can it wait?' She simply wasn't in the mood, wasn't up to one of Declan's let's-be-friends lectures. Sure, they could be, would be, friends, she was confident of that.

Just not today.

But Declan was adamant. 'No, Lila, it can't.'

Tossing her hot chocolate into a bin, she followed him the few steps to the courtyard, her courtyard, where she watched the sunrise, listened to the traffic. It would now for ever remind her of the day she'd lost the two people she cared most about.

'I took Yvonne out last night,' Declan started. His words were uneasy, his voice hesitant. 'We had a long talk over dinner and I told her—'

'I know you went out last night.' Lila took a deep breath. 'Look, Declan, this really isn't a good time for me right now. If you're happy with Yvonne then I'm happy for you, but I really don't need the details—'

'What are you going on about?' He seemed genuinely bemused. 'I told her about us.'

'Us?' Lila almost laughed. 'What *us*?'

'*This* us.' Placing the bouquet on the bench behind her, Declan took her face in his hands and kissed her gently, slowly, tenderly. Pulling back just an inch, his words were soft. 'The us that never would go away no matter how we fought it.

'I told Yvonne last night that she had to move out—not tomorrow or anything so dramatic but at least before your mother's discharged. I want you both to come and live with me.'

Lila shook her head, desperate to put him straight, positive that she must have somehow misheard. 'You don't understand…'

'I know I don't, Lila,' he rasped. His haste to reach her, to put things right once and for all made him impatient to continue. 'But I know that I love you, love everything about you. I've tried to get over you. I've tried for eight years and I can't. I've finally come to the conclusion that the reason I can't is quite simply because I'm not supposed to. We were meant for each other, Lila. And the more the years go by the more I see it. I'm sorry, so sorry if I caused you pain all that time ago. In my defence all I can say is that I didn't mean to.'

'I've hurt you, too,' Lila admitted, while scared to point out her faults as if somehow it might force Declan to retract the delicious words he was uttering. 'All the things you said about me not growing up, not supporting you…'

'Couples row, people say things when they're hurt. And I was hurt, Lila, so hurt. You wouldn't let me near you, wouldn't let me in. The only way you'd even consider accepting my help was if it was purely as a friend. The stuff about asking Yvonne out was just a guise, a guise to make you think I was over you. Then maybe you'd let me help you.'

'You're not sleeping with her?'

He laughed; he actually laughed at the very suggestion. 'No way. Whatever gave you that idea?'

'You did.' She was bemused, confused, but utterly giddy with love. 'When I woke up and you were gone, I heard you in her room. You told me—'

'What was I supposed to say, Lila? All that spiel I gave you about being friends didn't actually translate to sharing a bed with you. Yvonne's witch's den seemed a safer bet. Still, I moved like a scalded cat the second she came home. Hell, if I'd stayed there a moment longer I could have had a lawsuit against me.

'You still don't get it, do you? I love you, Lila. I love the passionate way you care for your family. And loving someone means helping them to fulfil their dreams. If you want to look after your mum at home then you will. We will,' he corrected himself. 'But properly and with help. We'll face it all together.'

She had waited so long to hear those words. Waited so long for a knight in shining armour to come along and lift her up, carry her clear from the

endless load she bore. And though it was too late for
Elizabeth, it wasn't too late for Lila. The imaginary
test, the hurdles she had put up—he had passed them
all.

Surpassed them even.

And when finally he let her speak, when she finally
told him the terrible news that had brought her out
there, he held her in his arms and cried with her.
Cried for Elizabeth and the sad, premature end to her
life, cried for his Lila and the pain she was feeling
and cried for all those wasted years.

'There is something we can do for your mum,' he
said finally, holding her even closer.

Trust Declan to come up with a solution.

Trust Declan to make the blackest day of her life
also the happiest.

Taking a seat by the bed a little later he held Lila's
hand as he spoke to Elizabeth. Told her that she
didn't have to worry, that Lila was going to all right,
more than all right. That he would be there for her,
take care of her, and always, always love her.

'I promise, Elizabeth, I'll make her happy.' Looking up, he smiled with love at the brave face of Lila.

'I let your beautiful daughter get away once and I
swear to you I'm never going to make the same mistake again.'

EPILOGUE

DECLAN took Lila to the Grampian Mountains. It seemed a strange choice for two such well-travelled people who had loved the glitz and glamour of sumptuous hotel rooms, marble bathrooms and five-star dinners.

But in Victoria's west, with rolling mountains and native fauna abounding, they were able to relax and let the beauty of nature at its finest soothe away the hurts of the past, invigorate them for the future.

Not that they roughed it. The Royal Mail Hotel was arguably one of the Grampians' finest, and they dined night after night in the luxury restaurant, returning to their chalet under the gentle gaze of the mountains, back to their tiny slice of heaven.

On their last day they packed a picnic and returned to their favourite walk, climbing the small Piccaninny Mountain, and once at the top they gazed down hand in hand, proud of their achievement, not just the walk but of making it together.

'I love you, Lila, I always have.'

Tears filled her eyes as she drank in the view, and as magnificent as it was she pulled her gaze away to a better one. To Declan. To the eyes that would now greet her each morning, the eyes that would gently bid her goodnight.

'I love you, too.' They were only words, easily said but heartfelt. And they still managed to take Lila by surprise when she uttered them.

She had always loved him, always, but now there was no shame, no embarrassment in admitting it.

'I don't want to go back to work,' she admitted. 'I really wanted the job but now that I've got it, it doesn't seem so important any more.'

'It will,' Declan said. 'Once you're back you'll fall in love with it all over again. It's just hard at the moment with all that you've been through. You couldn't not do it. For one thing you'd miss all the gossip too much if you left. Hey, how about Mr Hinkley and Yvonne finally getting together? I still can't get over that!'

Lila laughed. 'He did seem a bit keen at the staff party. Of course, Yvonne only had eyes for you then, but I'm sure the ground was laid then. She's not so bad really.'

Declan groaned. 'I guess. Actually, that party's got a lot to answer for: Yvonne and Mr Hinkley, Jez and Sue.' He kissed the top of her head. 'Well, good luck to them, I hope they're as happy as we are.'

Lila nodded. Slipping into his arms, she laid her head on his chest as she breathed in the fresh, still air.

'I'm a bit worried about the Horse, though,' Lila said thoughtfully. 'How she's going to take the news.'

A possum was climbing a tree just a few metres from them. The eternal townie, Declan was surprised how fascinating watching this tiny creature could be and he only half listened as Lila chatted away.

'What news?'

'You were right. The staff party does have a lot to answer for. Not only has the Horse blown fifty dollars from the budget by changing my name tags from Bailey to Haversham, now the new associate charge nurse is going to be taking maternity leave after only five minutes in the job.'

Declan stiffened in her arms, his breath suddenly still. Even the possum seemed to understand the magnitude of what was taking place and froze on the tree, his brown eyes staring widely at Lila.

'Say something,' Lila grumbled. Her cheeks were burning as she awaited his response.

'I know it's a bit soon, but say something,' she pleaded. 'Anything.'

Pulling her down on the soft grass beside him, Declan ran a lazy hand through her long blonde hair. 'What are you talking about—"it's a bit too soon"?' He kissed the hollows of her throat, wrapped his arms protectively around her. Pulling away, he gazed at her with love and adoration, the look in his eyes making Lila more dizzy than any multi-trauma ever could.

'What I was going to say, Mrs Haversham, if you'll ever let me get a word in edgeways, is, why on earth did we wait so long...?'

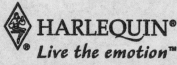

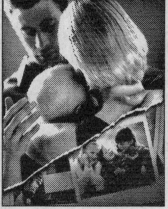
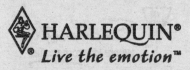

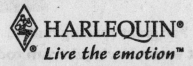